"Faithfully discreet servants and high-handed gentry may seem like the sole province of *Downton Abbey* and the like, but Jean Ayer exposes a new generation of scandal in the delightfully quirky *Dead Drunk*, set in the fictional seaside town of French Haven, Maine. Double gin martinis and dysfunction are served up in this breezy summer tale turned murder mystery. With honesty and insight, Ayer penetrates the glamorous facade of the wealthy "summer people" by revealing the tragic consequences of alcoholism over generations.

Richard has worked for George and Margaret Wollaston for more than a decade. He enjoys eccentric Aunt Beth's inscrutable ramblings, quietly entertains romantic notions toward Angie, and admires Margaret's classy demeanor. He is well known and well liked by the wealthy summer families: "Richard waits tables. He tends bar, he cooks, he'll fix your flowers, he'll go out in your garden and *pick* your flowers. He'll feed your dog; he'll climb a tree to get your cat down. Richard does everything." This particular summer, Richard will also discover the lifeless body of a Wollaston family member and be thrust into a surprising investigation encompassing both the upper crust and lower dregs of French Haven society.

Dead Drunk begins with a heartfelt introduction that sets the scene, tone, and background for the story, and also sheds light on the inspiration behind it. It is worth noting that the premise originated in Ayer's own experiences living with an alcoholic husband. The introduction is followed by a list of principal characters, reminiscent of the great American plays of the twentieth century. Chapter titles, including "George on the Porch," "Richard Upstairs," and "James and

Angie" add to the overall stage effect and even pacing found throughout. Ayer infuses the Wollastons' world with sights, sounds, tastes, and smells that virtually leap off the page.

Ayer handles serious topics such as alcoholism, verbal abuse, suicide, drug use, rebellion, and divorce with sensitivity and insight that add a level of believability to the characters. George's relationship with his wife, Margaret, and their children, Angie and Tony, is vivid in its complete breakdown, and it is easy to see how a beloved husband and father can become an adversary through years of alcohol abuse: "Laughter was his weapon, laced with irony and ridicule. He used his weapons thoughtlessly and thoroughly, seemingly unaware that the kids were too young to understand or defend themselves." Despite the gravity of emotions, Ayer keeps the tone light, allowing *Dead Drunk* to serve as both an enjoyable and a cautionary tale.

The novel is in turns sensitive and humorous, delving into the private lives and societal expectations surrounding the Wollaston clan. The town of French Haven is vividly drawn with sympathetic, evolving characters, yet the plot is filled with enough twists, turns, and sleuthing to satisfy those in search of a murder mystery. Consider filling the time between episodes of *Downton Abbey* with a copy of *Dead Drunk*."

—*Foreword Clarion Reviews*

"A fine murder mystery, in the style of Agatha Christie, with a hawk-eyed protagonist and bevy of suspects."

—*Kirkus Reviews*

Jean Ayer, a native of West Virginia, moved to New York City with a scholarship to Barnard College. After graduate work at Johns Hopkins School of Advanced International Studies, she qualified for the U.S. Foreign Service, but stayed in New York to work as a cartoonist and fashion illustrator. Her work appeared in *Esquire, Vogue*, The *New Yorker, Harper's Bazaar, Redbook, Mademoiselle, Town & Country,* and major New York newspapers. She also translated Portuguese and French for MacMillan, Abrams, Pocket Books, and Penguin.

She married a summer resident of Bar Harbor, Maine, where she raised a family from the 1950s into the '80s. During this time she transcribed her mother's stories of her childhood in West Virginia at the dawn of the twentieth century. These were later published, reworked as fiction, as *Tales of Chinkapin Creek* and *Tales of Chinkapin Creek, Volume II,* and are available from Amazon.com. Work on these stories got her started in writing, which she pursued vigorously after her divorce. She studied creative writing at the Virginia Center for the Creative Arts and various writers' associations, then attained an MFA in creative writing from Columbia University.

DEAD DRUNK

A novel by
Jean Ayer

ISBN: 1484980670
ISBN 13: 9781484980675
Library of Congress Control Number: 2013909616
CreateSpace Independent Publishing Platform
North Charleston, South Carolina

ACKNOWLEDGEMENTS...vii

INTRODUCTION ix

PRINCIPAL CHARACTERS xi

1   ALDERWOOD 1

2   EIGHT O'CLOCK 17

3   TEN O'CLOCK 33

4   GEORGE ON THE PORCH 45

5   IN THE SILENT HOUSE 53

6   RICHARD UPSTAIRS... 62

7   AFTER MIDNIGHT.. 69

8   JAMES'S STORY.. 75

9   SLEEPLESS NIGHT 85

10 RICHARD'S STATEMENT 93

11 RICHARD DRINKING.. 106

12 INTRUDERS 112

13 CLAMSHELLS 120

14 VISITING TIM 126

15 GEORGE'S LAST PARTY 134

16 A GOOD PLACE TO START 149

17 JAMES AND GEORGE 155

18 ELIOT COLLARS LUKE..................................... 164

19 LE BEL AT ALDERWOOD 170

20 ANGIE AND MRS. MONCURE 179

21 RICHARD RECONNOITERS............................... 189

22 LE BEL GOES VISITING 197

23 JAMES AND MARGARET 208

24 JAMES AND ANGIE 217

25 RICHARD SETS A TRAP 224

26 MRS. MONCURE'S NEW EYRIE 230

27 THE TEA PARTY 236

28 RICHARD AND FLORA...................................... 242

29 RICHARD AT ELIOT'S 250

30 RICHARD AND MARGARET............................... 256

ACKNOWLEDGEMENTS

Without the hard work, unwavering support, and encouragement of my son Bob Ayer and my friend and assistant Kevin Meredith, this book would not have been possible.

I would also like to thank my wonderfully gifted sister Ann Van Saun and my talented nephew Kyle Van Saun for their amazing insights and suggestions along the way. I'm indebted to the following writers, aka "The Group": Myriam Chapman, Judi Culbertson, Teresa Giordano, Adele Glimm, Tom House, Eleanor Hyde, Harriet LaBarre, Elizabeth Jakab, Carol Pepper, Maureen Sladen, and Marcia Slatkin.

INTRODUCTION

This is a novel set in a summer resort town on the coast of Maine. The old rich are deeply entrenched, and the natives are as deeply resentful. The tourists are curious about what goes on in those big houses. It would be a Maine version of an *Upstairs Downstairs* sort of story except that the old-fashioned "proper" ways are mere memories by the 1980s. Still, the descendants of the "old guard" have their own ways of doing things. They display a certain nonchalance regarding the unexpected death of one of their own and the subsequent police investigation. This is a detective story as well as a candid look behind the façade of a troubled family. These days it would be called a *dysfunctional family*, but new terms are usually viewed with suspicion, as is anything else that's new, in such a tradition-bound community.

Having raised a family in Maine, the author studied creative writing, with the objective of puzzling out the chain of events that led to and followed her divorce. She wrote short stories of fiction based on the progression of alcoholism in her former husband and its crippling effects on their family. The stories inspired further work on the seemingly inscrutable mystery of why her marriage fell apart. Her work on the problem was informed by her participation in Al-anon and related programs. Fiction allowed her to weave the elements together into an intriguing mystery: this novel is the surprising result of her quest.

The foundation of the story was drawn from the latter years of the author's marriage. Her son, in his teenage years at the time, was a contributing editor. He added his own perspective, which gave the children their own voice in the face of the depredations of a capricious father.

PRINCIPAL CHARACTERS

GEORGE	father
MARGARET	mother
ANGIE	daughter
TONY	son
MRS. MONCURE	Margaret's aunt
MISS HARDY	George's aunt
LYLE	George's brother
ENID	Lyle's wife
PRIS	George's cousin
LUCASTA, BEA, BILLY, TOAD	drinking buddies
RICHARD	accommodating barman
JAMES	native friend of Angie
ELIOT	Chief of Police
LE BEL	State Police Detective
FLORA	a waitress
DERMOTT	a local yokel

I

ALDERWOOD

Richard spills his groceries as he jumps out of the way of an old red truck, rumbling by in the parking lot in front of the Shop 'n' Save. He shouts after it, "Hey, *Dermott*! You almost hit me!"

The round, red brake lights shine. The truck rumbles back to stop beside him. Husky, red-faced Dermott, with his flat-topped crew cut, revs the poorly muffled engine as he glares down at Richard from the high cab. For emphasis he lets off the gas — BAAAAGH — enough to make Richard jump. There's nothing new in Dermott's caustic look, only a faint glint of what Richard suspects may be amusement. After another uneasy moment of staring at each other, Dermott thunders off, letting out another BAAAAGH!

Someone comes running up saying, "I saw it. It looked like he *meant* to do it."

Surely that's an exaggeration, Richard thinks...but then he wouldn't be surprised, especially after *this* episode, if Dermott turned out to be one to carry a grudge.

Richard will worry about Dermott later. For the moment he has to gather up his groceries, replace anything that's broken, and hurry on home. He has a considerable amount of preparation to do for tonight's dinner party at Alderwood.

ၭ ၭ ၭ

Alderwood is one of several "cottages" that survived the great fire in French Haven, Maine, many years ago. Rambling old mansions with loose window locks and glass-paned doors, their skeleton keys dangle from inside keyholes. Alderwood is perhaps the grandest of those that remain, with thirty rooms set back in the woods and a billion-dollar view. The cottages are occupied, for two or three months out of the year, by the vacationing wealthy from New York, Philadelphia, and other cities. Many of the locals live off these "summer people" in their big cottages as well as the tourists who stay briefly in hotels and such. The locals dislike, or at least distrust, both groups.

To reach the Wollastons' cottage, you drive through the village of French Haven on what the locals still call the Old Cape Road. You pass the ball field, then an old carriage house that Buddy Smalley is turning into condominiums. A mile out on the ocean side, you come to a driveway flanked by a pair of carved stone pillars. A varnished wooden sign, black lettering on clear yellow pine, announces the cottage's name: "ALDERWOOD." A bigger sign, labeled "PRIVATE," hangs from the bottom edge of the first. A third sign, very large, has been added about ten feet past the entrance. It says, "KEEP OUT."

The "incident," that prompted the two largest signs to be put up, occurred years ago. Kids from all over the country converged on French Haven. They took any road, path, driveway, or gap in a fence they could find to get to the beach. Often they strode right across the Wollastons' lawn. The trespassing didn't make Margaret Wollaston feel any warmer toward the public.

ﶂ ﶂ ﶂ

Much more than a mere caterer, Richard does a little of everything. Cook sick? Get Richard. Got no cook? Get Richard, say members of the summer colony. Richard waits tables. He tends bar, he cooks, he'll fix your flowers, he'll go out in your garden and *pick* your flowers. He'll feed your dog; he'll climb a tree to get your cat down. Richard does everything.

Richard the reliable: silent, honest, incurious, discreet, and invisible, a servant in the style of the old school, a dying breed. He feels a twinge of irritation at this image of himself. He's only twenty-nine. What would his father have said if he'd lived to see his only son wearing a monkey suit and serving fancy food to the rich?

Richard remembers when Alderwood's driveway gravel was rose-colored granite pea stone, inches thick and raked every day. Now its surface is hard as cement, and the only remaining loose gravel is at the edges. The property was once tended by a large grounds crew. Now it lies neglected, intermittently mown, with weeds and fallen branches littering the great lawn. The once-grand arrangement of lilac, mock-orange, sweetbriar, and Norway maple has been left to tangle. Untrimmed, the place has the feel of an abandoned estate. A dead oak that fell four or five years ago, barely missing the cottage, has been left to rot.

The last time Richard came to work here was last summer, and the current summer is all but past. As he drives in, he sees a kid lounging against a light-starved old apple tree. Wearing a T-shirt that says "NEW DAY SAME OLD SHIT," the kid appears to be smoking pot. The weather is scorching; the woods are dry as tinder.

The inner driveway, marked with a "SERVICE" sign, is blocked by an old Porsche. A litter of oil cans and tools surrounds it. A pair of skinny, grease-stained legs sticks out from under the rusted car. George Wollaston's daughter, she's eighteen but looks fourteen.

Richard rolls down his window. "Hey, Angie."

"Hey, Richaahd," she says in the accent she puts on when she summers in Maine.

He turns off his Subaru, opens the hatchback, and pulls out his equipment. He's the only barman in French Haven who wears a white mess jacket cut in the old style. It's what every waiter at the French Haven Club used to wear, starched so stiff it crackles faintly when he moves. He ties his own black bow tie.

"Somebody coming to help you out tonight, Richaahd?"

He pauses to think. "Flora," he says.

4

Angie rolls out from under the Porsche on an orange plastic creeper. There's grease on her nose and chin, in her blonde hair, and on her once-white T-shirt. She's a pretty girl, and she has a wonderful, real smile for him. "Guess what, Richaahd? I'm going to eat with the *grownups* tonight. Going to talk bridge with Billy, get pinched by Toad, going to hear Lucasta tell who she knows and what they've done." She scratches her ankle. "But maybe I can sit with Aunt Beth. What're you giving us to eat this time?"

Richard pauses again. He works in so many houses. "Ah...Jellied madrilene. Filet of beef, peas in artichoke hearts. Ah...grilled tomatoes. Lemon soufflé. Ah...paté and raw stuff with the drinks."

"In that case I might just get through the ordeal," she says. "You wouldn't have time to help me out with the car, would you?"

Richard always has time for Angie. He has had a crush on her for years, and she is not indifferent to him. But she's always been a minor, and while Angie is inclined to flout a law for the fun of it, Richard is not. Angie often hangs around here, tinkering with the Porsche.

"Park the wagon for me," he says. "I'll just take my things in first."

The hands of the kitchen clock, above the pitted soapstone sink, point to four o'clock. Richard deposits his jacket on a wire hanger inside the door. He sets his bag and cooler on the big oiled oak table. He checks the serving pantry to see what instructions Angie's mother has left for him. He finds an untidy scrap of paper on the narrow ledge that fronts a row of varnished matchboard cupboards. He tucks it into his pocket and goes back into the kitchen. He finds comfort in the familiar gesture of shaking out his apron and putting it on.

He unpacks his bag. First out are the shallow-bordered silver trays and sauce boats with serving spoons. His reliable old Solingen carving knives with a carborundum sharpening steel have chased-silver ferrules and stag horn handles. His bar tools include pincers for breaking ice cubes without spattering fragments around. To a man like Richard, who had so little stability in his past, antique objects represent reassurance and comfort — even, however spuriously, heritage.

Using his own things saves scrambling every day — twice a day at this time of year — in a different big cupboard or pantry in some different enormous summer cottage. The silver pieces clink as he sets them down. He has collected most of them at cottage sales, as the older generation of French Haven's summer colony dies off. Their big old places are then torn down or converted into hotels, religious retreats, conference centers, or, lately, condominiums. George Wollaston would be surprised to know that Richard's pair of heavy Tiffany Olympia serving forks once belonged to his own great-grandmother. The bag itself, of supple old calfskin crusted over with faded CUNARD stickers, made the grand tour with that same ancestor.

The last item Richard unpacks is a packet of place cards — not a usual accessory for him to provide, but Alderwood is no longer a usual place for him to work. Since Tony's death, any number of items have needed Richard's attention, things the old Margaret Wollaston never would have neglected.

The cooler holds groceries. Unpacking it, he takes the time to find a pan for the filet and set the vegetables aside for Flora to deal with.

When he goes out to get his second cooler, Angie has moved his Subaru and the Porsche as well. She sits on the rickety old slatted oak swing where her family's Irish maids once cooled their heels.

"You'll be glad to hear I don't need your help now, Richaahd," she says. "Sit down, take a load off. Luke helped me."

"Luke?" Richard drags up a sagging wicker chair.

"Luke's a creep the old man hired. Don't bother to look — you won't see him. You know potheads. You've heard Dad's lecture, I hope? The kid's stoned out of his mind. He deals the stuff, but Dad thinks he's a model boy. Wears shoes, combs his hair: voilà, the old man's kind of kid." She gives a push that sends her swinging away. "Myself when young," she adds.

She was a lovely child, Richard remembers. Green eyes heavily fringed with dark lashes, blonde hair that's darkening now. "Isn't he working a little late, this Luke?" he asks, a touch of jealousy evident in his tone.

"Oh, he has his own schedule. Dad gives him a list. He works when he can fit it in, or so he says."

"Fit in to what?"

She widens her eyes at him. "Richaahd, you surprise me."

"Well, fit in to what?"

"I told you. He deals. Here's how Dad hired him. He put an ad in the paper. Luke took off his nose rings, cut his shoulder-length hair, and answered the ad. Oh, was Dad ever taken in! 'You look like a fine young fellow. You'll do.' Showed him all around. 'This is my wife, here's my daughter, over there's where we keep the booze, in here's the silver, upstairs first door to the right is where my wife keeps her jewelry.' No references. Mom was *livid*."

A wood thrush sings its end-of-day song. Richard and Angie listen to the liquid, descending notes: *ee-oh-lay*. When it falls silent, Richard asks, "What're your plans, Angie?"

She gives him a wry look. "Auto-mechanics school. I told Dad, and you'd have thought I said training camp for commie pinko guerrilla terrorists. 'Is that what your mother and I sent you to Saint Tim's for?' he shouted. 'I should've known what would come of your taking a year out, traipsing round the country with those *hippies*!' Man, he was pissed!"

She studies her fingernails, rimmed with grease. "Oh well. He pays, I go where he says...maybe. My idea is that Dad never left the marines. To him Mom and I are just recruits. My brother was a recruit who didn't make it. Those meetings help you only so much, you know. The reason I go is because they help Mom."

Al-Anon, she means. The meetings are held in the basement of the Congregational Church.

Angie gives the swing a violent push that sends her racketing away. "There's a limit," she says. Swinging back, she eyes Richard coolly.

"How about your friend James?" he asks.

She laughs. "You may see him tonight. He'll be down here around midnight."

The French Haven Police Department checks around the summer places during the night. James is a summer cop. His uncle Eliot, the local chief, has taken him on as a reserve officer for the summer. In Richard's dozen years in French Haven, he's come to know James. He seems to be a nice kid, tall, reserved, and mostly silent. James and Angie, both troubled souls, find comfort in each other's company.

A breeze springs up. The pale aspen leaves flutter, and the solitary wood thrush calls again: *ee-oh-lay*. Richard waits for it to still, then pushes off from his creaking chair and gets to his feet.

"Come in and keep me company, Angie. You realize I don't make this offer to every daughter of the house where I work."

"Look for me in the drawing room. Ta ta," she says, imitating the fashionable summer girls. She gives the swing another vicious push and leers down at him over her shoulder.

On his way back to the kitchen, Richard passes through a maze of small rooms overflowing with junk of every description. These are the former servants' rooms. Sitting room, dining room, housekeeper's study, laundry, and spaces for uses long forgotten, they were once neat and suitably furnished. Now they're chockablock with old garden tools, broken clam rakes and hods, weather-beaten croquet mallets, beach towels smelling of mice, chairs with missing legs, ancient wicker rug beaters, and sail bags gray with age. Most fitting of all amongst this flotsam of a shipwrecked family is a life-size, inflated rubber mermaid someone gave George years ago as a joke. Empty liquor bottles are everywhere.

At the kitchen table Richard draws out a chair and flattens Margaret's scrap of paper. In most of the cottages, he expects to find a note from his employer or her cook (much of his work comes on cooks' nights out). At Alderwood there always used to be such a note, an enthusiastic composition that gave him pleasure.

"Richard, the kids picked beach peas this morning, look out back in the flower sink. What do you think of them for a centerpiece? How about the Copenhagen seagull plates?" Her instructions in those days included a careful seating diagram. She chose her guests carefully too: besides the French Haven summer regulars, she sometimes had someone very young or very old or with unexpected credentials. In George's set, though, anyone might show up. Once he invited a couple of trespassers he met on the beach. They claimed to be walking from Cape Ann to the Gaspé Peninsula.

Richard used to find Margaret's thick, creamy, crimson-monogrammed cards, inscribed in her firm handwriting, neatly stacked beside her diagram. She left high-spirited bouquets on tables polished till he could see his face in the deep, rich grain of the wood. He finds it hard now to reconcile the woman who wrote those cards with the woman who has scrawled barely legibly on this torn paper scrap that looks as if it has been used to wrap meat: "Guests at 7:30. Ten at table. Sit down 8:30." Names, scribbled negligently around a lopsided circle, represent a party of ten. Six he recognizes as family members, the others as hard-drinking sidekicks of George. The party was George's idea, as well as the guest list. George telephoned Richard to make the date — Tuesday, August thirtieth — the first party at Alderwood all summer. In years past, this house regularly saw four or five bashes a season, with a dozen servants and all the front rooms full of tables. George's special pleasure was live music: he usually had singers with a string trio or sometimes a whole band.

Money is not the problem. What's gone out of this household is the energy that has seeped out of Margaret since her son's suicide. That broke her spirit beyond repair. He'd been so young and full of life. She adored him, held out such hope for him. When the news came, all she could do was sit down, struck dumb. She blames his father, George. Everyone blames George — except George himself of course.

"Fine then," he said at the time. "If he can't take a little constructive criticism, then he wouldn't have lasted long in this world anyway. It's cruel to say, but there it is."

Richard takes the place cards from their package and a fountain pen from his pocket. He writes, in a large hand that he hopes the farsighted and intoxicated can read by candlelight, a card for each family member: Margaret, George,

Angie, Aunt Beth, Enid, and Pris. George's sister-in-law, Enid, stays at her cottage next door. He writes the remaining cards for George's pick of his drinking buddies: Bea, Toad, Lucasta, and Billy.

In the serving pantry, Richard takes down a tray and chooses the ten least damaged plates from dozens of old Derby, Chelsea, Minton, Mason, and Copenhagen stock. He then continues into the dining room.

"Good evening, Robin."

This is Margaret Wollaston's aunt, Mrs. Moncure, dressed in a frilly, lime green evening dress. A Southerner, judging by her drawl, she has her own name for everyone. Something faintly Southern lingers in Margaret's speech too. Some kind of crisis in Margaret's family, Richard figures, has caused the old lady to descend on her. Last summer he overheard telephone conversations. Margaret met her at the bus station. He can imagine how the old lady might cause a crisis. She talks nonstop. Each time he worked here last year she discovered his presence early and talked to him (rather at him), carrying on until it was time for him to leave. She followed him around, hands folded at her waist, her green eyes (like the young Vivien Leigh, she often pointed out) sad and remote. She moved into the servants' wing at the back of the house, however odd that seemed, especially since it was her own choice.

"I do hope my being here won't trouble you, Robin," she says. One of her small hands drifts from her waist to the dining room table. She runs her fingers back and forth along the edge of the wood, making a faint squeak. It's one of her odd habits. She always wears some flowery perfume; this evening it's roses. Richard assures her she is no trouble. Squeak, squeak, squeak. "Mr. Moncure was not a perfectionist. He never had patience with that quality in me. Indeed he did *not*."

Last year, when he wasn't too busy, Richard amused himself by trying to puzzle out her non sequiturs. Once he discovered she didn't expect answers, he found her presence soothing. She has a lovely musical voice, low-pitched and sweetly modulated. Her babble is as monotonous as a brook running unceasingly over pebbles. He has never heard her laugh.

"What do you believe in, Robin?" Squeak, squeak, squeak, like an un-rosined bow rubbing a catgut string. He has to step around her as he works.

"You mean do I believe in God, Mrs. Moncure? I believe in God, I think."

He leaves the tray, with the place cards and Margaret's diagram, for Flora to deal with. Stepping again around Mrs. Moncure, he surveys the sideboard and makes a mental note to have Flora polish the candlesticks.

"Do you believe in happiness, Robin? Everyone should be happy. It is very important."

"Of course I believe in happiness, Mrs. Moncure."

Flora has arrived. Through the open window he hears the old truck's raucous sputter, like that of an ancient, used-up Model A Ford.

"Everyone is entitled to be happy and live in peace." Mrs. Moncure's hand keeps rubbing the wood. "That is the essential, do you not agree, Robin?"

Without answering, he steps around her and pushes through the swinging door on his way to the kitchen.

Flora is just shrugging off her sweater. She is small and thin, what for a lady in George's circle would be called *petite*. She shakes out a white cotton work apron to protect the crisp, organdy version she wears when she's serving. Then she fishes in her pocketbook for a crushed pack of Marlboros. Richard feels he should speak with her on the subject of the smell of tobacco on a woman who serves food. Not tonight, and not in this house. She is useful to him, but she's prickly. And then he has an odd foreboding. He watches her find an ashtray.

"What's it this time, Richard?" she says.

He tells her the menu, adding, "The madrilene is canned, in the big refrigerator."

A whoosh of air comes from the swinging pantry door. It's Mrs. Moncure. "Getting the job done somehow was Mr. Moncure's way," she says as the door bats behind her. "He believed it a waste of time to trouble over details. Oh, he was a *scamp*!" She begins a series of little stitching motions in the air with her fingertips as if she holds a needle.

Flora rolls her eyes at Richard. Ashtray in hand, she makes a tour of the kitchen and pantry. She too works in a different house every night. Within minutes she is back. Setting down her ashtray, she hunts in a drawer for a knife. Richard is amazed that she always finds a sharp one. Her first job is to sort and wash the vegetables.

"Who they having?" she asks.

He tells her, "Ten, counting the six of them."

"Six of them?"

"Enid Wollaston's here."

"Uh-oh." Flora makes an unpleasant face. "Who's number ten?"

"Angie."

"Godfrey! What's the point of *that*? What's she want, sittin' down with that bunch?"

"Maybe George wants to test whether she's settled down or not."

Flora shakes her head as she unwraps broccoli, tomatoes, and radishes. She dumps them in the sink and turns on the cold water. She raises her voice over the water's roar. "I'm stayin' to help you clean up tonight, Richard."

He doesn't bother to comment. He knows that at the first sound of her husband's truck returning, she'll bolt. She is full of quirks. She hates the rich. She hates tourists, summer people, and the lawyers and doctors with their houses in among the summer properties on Water Street. She holds it against Richard that he wasn't born a native, that he receives — as the barman who hired her — a higher fee than she does, that he is a man, has an education, and owns a house.

Flora rarely puts her feelings into words. Richard senses them from clues she tosses out as she works. He likes her well enough though. She is the best worker he knows. In a pinch, he can count on her. As for calling the Wollastons "George" and "Margaret" to their faces, that's Maine. At least it's this part of Maine, where the rich have been entrenched for generations and the natives have devised their own ways of getting back at them.

Richard finds it unprofessional, the French Haven native's insistence on first-naming everyone. He considers Flora's smoking to be unprofessional as well. The odor of tobacco on her person interferes with the people's ability to appreciate the delicate flavor of his béarnaise, among other dishes. He closes his mind to the problem — for now at least.

"How's Dermott?" That's her husband.

She whirls on him as if stung, squints at him for a moment, then, as though remembering something, turns back. "Dermott's all right," she mutters. With her small knife, she carves a radish into a rose.

Mrs. Moncure, with her sad, remote expression, watches from her station near the pantry door. "I often reminded Mr. Moncure that everyone deserves to be happy and live in peace, indeed I did, often and often, but he was a *rascal*."

2

EIGHT O'CLOCK

When Richard was seventeen, he arrived in French Haven from a simple, small village in Nova Scotia. He found work at the French Haven Club, which caters to the wealthy summer people. He was dazzled by the rambling old clubhouse, alight in all its richly furnished downstairs rooms, redolent of the perfumes of fresh flowers. He enjoyed watching the candlelit dinner dances through the peephole in the pantry door.

Richard remembers Margaret from those days. A lady of about thirty-five, she impressed him as glamorous. He had a crush on her, and on her and George as a couple; they seemed a romantic pair.

His mentor, Crawford, had started in his thirties as barman at the club. He increasingly took jobs tending bar in the cottages, as well. By the time Richard came to work at the club, Crawford had long ago set up on his own but continued to tend bar at the club. In order to quit so he could go at it full time in the cottages, he'd have to train a new barman. He was so fussy that for years he rejected all prospects — until Richard showed up. Crawford took him on his cottage jobs too, and it wasn't long before Richard learned enough to help with Crawford's new sideline: catering.

Richard stayed on at the club and helped Crawford on the side as the need arose. Gradually, over the years, the need increased until Richard found himself too busy and had to give up his job at the club. He was soon busier than ever, however, as Crawford allowed him more responsibility. Crawford then married Kitty, his old sweetheart from his early days at the club. He thereafter encouraged Richard to take over the business.

At the cottages Richard found himself listening for the ring of Margaret's light voice, to be aware of where in the crowd she moved. She kept her luster well into her forties.

Margaret has always been a mystery to Richard. He likes her well enough but has never been able to understand why she travels with the people she does. Why did she marry George and why, in these last years, has she not left him? The answer might be sex: sparks sometimes pass between them, fiery enough to singe cloth. Although, it occurs to him, he has not seen anything like that for the last several years. It used to be that in a crowd of people it was all they could do to keep their hands off each other. Richard marvels, wondering if someday a woman will look at him like that. Sex must be it then, and George's undoubted charm... and perhaps the children.

Margaret was an indifferent mother to her children. She was so absorbed with George and his world that she didn't have much left for them. It seems to Richard that, same as his own father, George had let them down; so she was all they had. Nursemaids, au pairs, and tutors had brought them up, yet they were loyal to their mother. She must have given them a good measure of caring attention, a merciful respite perhaps from George's negligence. Margaret invariably deals with Richard as an individual, not a faceless provider of services. Surely the children saw more than her good manners and graceful ability to deal with people.

Richard remembers overhearing Margaret say, "I'll hold your hand, I'll stand by you, however long it takes. I'll do anything. This is no way to live."

George replied, his strong voice sounding stiff and offended, "I don't know what you mean."

The old heat ducts carried the sounds straight from the front of the house to the laundry, where Richard had gone to find a rag. He stood transfixed, unable to carry on about his business. That would have been the decent, professional thing to do, but he was intrigued enough to be carried away.

"What are you talking about, 'No way to live?'" George said. "You and I have everything anybody could want. You have everything a woman could want. You say I've changed. I'm the same man I've always been." Then George's voice turned suspicious, accusing. "There's something I have to tell *you*, Margaret. *You're* the one who's changed. *You're* the one who's different. Don't think people don't notice. Something's eating you, but it beats me. We have this house and the house in New York, we have the boat, we have friends, we take great trips…"

Margaret's voice burst out, with an anguished break clearly audible to Richard through the heat vent in the floor as well as through the halls of the house. It was an odd double echo. The reverberations, tinny from the ducts below, and cavernous through the open doorway, combined in spooky, emphatic stereo. "Oh George, I love you! I want to help! Let's not fight! Please, George! Oh please, please, please!"

In the last few years, she has moved about her world in an increasingly dazed manner. She has aged markedly, assuming an air of fatigue and bewilderment. Perhaps she's found herself in a position she did not anticipate, could not understand. By her countenance she seems angry and perhaps even fearful.

Richard's mother wore that same look, all the more painful to Richard because he knew how desperately she hoped. Her hope was that things would get better, that his father, Andrew, would change his drunken ways. His parents fought in his presence until he was relegated to the uncertain care of an indifferent grandfather on a remote shore of the Maritimes.

§ § §

Richard presents his tray so the double gin martini in the big bucket glass will be handy to the lean, deeply tanned man standing by the fireplace with his arm ranging along the mantle. George Wollaston wears a lightweight plaid jacket, khaki trousers, and the carpet slippers he often shows off at parties. They are adorned with scenes done in needlepoint of a sailboat on one foot and a skier on the other, made for him by his wife, Margaret. He has the kind of pleased, expectant look a little kid might wear at Christmas.

"How's every little thing, Richard old man?" he asks, grinning. He sets down his empty glass and helps himself to the refill.

Richard finds it hard not to like Mr. Wollaston. "Fine, sir," he says.

Richard gives the tray a quarter turn. Margaret Wollaston accepts her weak Campari and soda. A pretty woman, about forty-five, suntanned and fit, she wears a short skirt and sleeveless shirt, turquoise and white. The red-orange afterglow of sunset, flooding into the room, subdues the lines on her unhappy face and lends her a deceptive glow. She absently takes the glass. She lifts it to her lips in the same preoccupied way.

Martini for the tall woman in yellow linen, George's cousin, Pris Armbrister. Tall, aristocratic and a little bucktoothed, she has the great dark eyes of a fawn. Her jolly face is softened by a lifetime of too much alcohol. Richard is fond of her and her affable style. She doesn't say much; in conversation, her usual response is a giggle.

He also likes her friend Bea Bassett, the short, stumpy woman in the silk coolie coat who arrived with her. Bea reminds Richard of an ageing street tough, complete with a raspy smoker's voice. The two attended the same schools, came out in the same season, were maids of honor at each other's wedding, and lost husbands within months of each other. All George's friends grew up playing in the same sandbox, so to speak.

For Bea, a double bourbon without water in another heavy bucket glass. She grins and says slyly, "Scene of the crime, eh, Richard?"

Scotch on the rocks for Toad Cordwainer, scotch without ice for Billy Abt. Toad is tall and stocky with a wide mouth, protruding eyes, and a bulbous nose. Billy, with his narrow, rather plain face, is short and rotund; he stands as tall as Toad's shoulder. Both dressed in light-colored, summer-weight suits, the one is a bachelor and the other an abandoned husband. Both are among the summer colony's preeminent extra men, all of whom are possessed of acceptable blood lines and the abilities to deal in small-talk, play bridge for high stakes, and hold their liquor. They are often invited to parties to balance the ever-increasing number of unattached women, due to the ravages of divorce and death.

Crawford had nicknames for all of them — behind their backs of course: Toad was "Don'tcha Know;" Billy was "Fido;" Pris and Bea, "Les Girls." Richard has his own nicknames for Les Girls: Pris is "Giggles" and Bea is "Don't tread on me."

For George's sister-in-law, in her plain purple dress, white wine. "You and I Understand Each Other" was

Crawford's name for Enid Wollaston. Between her prominent cheekbones and wide jaw, her hollow cheeks remind
Richard of the waist of an hourglass. His mother would
have called her "lantern-jawed." Enid is a small woman
with the single-minded moody look of someone who bears
a grudge. Her demeanor seems pinched, held in and watch-
ful. As far as Richard can see, her peers don't like her.

"How *are* you, Richard?" she asks in her little-girl
voice. "It's *so* nice to see you. Have you had a good year?"

Her husband is George's brother, Lyle, a Washington
lawyer who hasn't yet arrived in French Haven. He makes a
point of coming weeks after she does. They own the cottage
next door, which Crawford used to call "Outer Mongolia."

Richard used to imagine the children his employers
and their guests had been. Enid would have been the one
the other children forgot to invite, Margaret the popular
one she envied. Enid would have had a crush on George,
the popular boy with his clique of friends. Pris would have
been the serene, shy little girl and Bea, the tyke none of the
other children could bully.

Moving with his tray among George's guests, Richard
remembers Crawford, the old man with parsley on his breath
to hide the evidence of his last drink. Crawford claimed,
with his correct black coat and deadpan face, to have been
the head houseman at the British embassy in Washington.
Crawford taught Richard a few surprising technicalities of
his trade. "The people who furnished these old cottages put
mirrors everywhere. See? There and over there, and there.
Strategic, every one of them. You never thought of that,

did you?" The mirrors were intended, according to Crawford, not for hostesses to check their guests or to emphasize the proportions of a room but for the *servants*. Glass need refilling? A course at dinner removed? Somebody dropped a napkin? In mirrors a man like Crawford, and now Richard, can see it all without seeming to spy.

In the Venetian mirror over the fireplace, Richard watches Lucasta Forbush arrive, wearing a fancy red gown. Tall, well made and made up, she could be thirty or fifty, depending on one's point of view. The summer colony's foremost hostess, she pauses critically on the threshold before surging through the room.

"*Giorgio.*" She gives George an airy kiss. "*Maggie.*" Another kiss. "*Dear* hearts, have you any *idea* how *long* it is since I've *been* in this house? I couldn't even remember which *driveway* was yours! Finally I just drove in next door, and Enid's nice maid said why not park there and *walk* through. However, I persevered, and here I am. I parked out by the beech tree. I *hope* that's all right."

Richard imagines Lucasta's silver BMW, left in some inconsiderate position, blocking everything. Her martini is served differently at her request, in an enormous stemmed glass with a sprig of mint. She takes it from his tray, lifts her chin, flares her nostrils, and fixes him with her great, pale blue-gray eyes.

"At *least* Mrs. Wollaston's got *you*, Richard." She turns to address everyone in turn, as though *she* were the hostess, "But *Maggie*, dear heart, you *should* have taken the trouble to scare up more *men* for this party. By the bye you're looking a little off your *feed*, Maggie... Are you all *right*? Giorgio, you men can't just talk amongst your*selves*. Let's mix it up. Poor Enid's all *alone* over there... And look at that *hen* party on the sofa." Thus she shuffles them up, sending her host off to join his sister-in-law and Billy to sit with Bea and Pris. For herself she corners Toad.

Richard's name for her is "Lucy," after the bossy little friend of Charley Brown in the comic strip.

Mrs. Moncure, next to Richard, gravely watches all this. Lucasta turns back: she has forgotten to include Margaret's aunt. "Mrs. Moncure, I'm Lucasta Forbush," she says, "*You* remember *me*."

Richard feels Mrs. Moncure's attention equally on himself and this colorful guest. He wins: she turns to him as though to resume a conversation after a tedious interruption. "On the North Cape cruise, Robin, Mr. Moncure and I were the only passengers to get off in Finland. The remainder of the passengers continued on to Leningrad. Mr. Moncure was never seasick. I was, dreadfully, and he *did* tease me."

The colorful light intensifies the dark oak of the enormous living room's ancient Jacobean furniture. The air smells of lemon peel and bourbon and old sun-rotted curtains. Occasionally one gets a whiff of the paté, which Flora passes on a silver tray with linen napkins, and the toothed, quilted mint in Lucasta's glass.

Richard pauses to consider: roast out of the oven, rolls and tomatoes in the warming closet, soup chilled, lemons cut, horseradish sauce done. It's eight-twenty. Where's Angie?

Here she comes. She's changed into a sheer Indian print dress. In the reddening light, she too is transformed. George lifts his chin. The others turn their heads.

Silence.

Abruptly George barks, "*You* know better than to come in here dressed like *that*, Angela Wollaston!"

What's wrong with her dress? Richard wonders. He remembers his own father, wearing clerical robes, on a Sunday morning in the vestry bright with winter sunlight. "Don't come in here dressed like *that*, boy!" he exclaimed in his authoritative voice.

Pris holds out a welcoming hand. "Angie, dear, how are you?"

George glances around the room, then fixes his glare on Angie. "Don't you have any *regular* clothes?"

The girl's eyes pleadingly seek her mother.

"George..." Margaret says.

"Don't 'George' me," he fires back, without taking his eyes off Angie. "Is this what you want, Margaret, is this what you approve of?"

"Keep it up, George," says Margaret with bitter irony. "You want *her* to kill herself *too*?"

"*Hey!*" George roars. "Don't start in on me about *that*! My son didn't have the mettle to make it in this world. It would have happened anyway!"

Angie rolls her eyes and bends down to kiss Pris, who's sitting on the sofa. "I'm fine, Cousin Pris."

"By God, Angie, where do you think you are?" George demands. "On the town dock with some of your hippie friends? Look at how your cousin Pris is dressed. Look at what Lucasta's wearing! And you have the nerve to embarrass me by showing up dressed like *that*? Go to your room!" The blood has drained from George's face, most notably around his eyes and nose: he looks like a raccoon.

Angie takes a quick step backward as soon as he begins his tirade...then she can't move. All she can do is stand there and weather the storm. *But what's the point?* she screams to herself in anguish. She's all too familiar with her father's marine drill-sergeant face in her face, yelling, "Don't you talk back to me, young lady!" After he has a moment to deflate a bit, he usually adds in a less forceful tone, "You should be *ashamed* of yourself." She feels a rush of pressure surge through her face, and her ears ring. She wishes she could disappear from this scene. *From this **life**,* she adds vehemently.

Her indignation fairly screams to be heard or at least recognized, yet she's learned that there's no help for it. The only relief is to retreat into her old, familiar, got-it-together persona. She tells the world, "I'm fine"...on the surface anyway.

Angie ambles through the room and addresses her father's guests with a small voice. "Good night, Cousin Pris. Goodnight, Mrs. Bassett. Mr. Abt... Mr. Cordwainer... Mrs. Forbush... Aunt Beth... Aunt Enid." Angie pauses on the threshold of the open French doors, her thin figure framed in the red light.

"But I thought you were dining with us tonight," protests Pris, hauling herself unsteadily to her feet. "I was *so* looking forward to it."

"I thought so too," replies Angie, "but I didn't know there was a dress code. Night, Daddy," she says cheerily. "Night, Mom. So long, all." She steps out onto the porch. In the mirror, Richard sees her unlatch the gate atop the steep stairs leading down to the lawn. She quickly drops from sight.

Angie lets gravity take her, descending the steps at a weightless run. Stepping onto the lawn, she feels relieved to be delivered from yet another of her father's attacks. She sings a refrain she learned from a friend she met at Al-Anon. As Aretha Franklin sings, "Chain, chain, chain..." so Angie sings, "Shame, shame, shame..." It helps to dispel the rage she used to feel as she so often went storming blindly away.

Richard's stomach flutters. He wants to follow her. He wants to find her in the woods and tell how he feels about her. She's said she feels the same about him. Now she's eighteen, and the two of them could...

"Richard! Another martini," George calls. Richard has no choice: he must answer.

Traces of white still show against George's tan, on either side of his nose and mouth. He sits abruptly.

Bea, on her spindly legs, stoops in front of him. She bends down and peers into his eyes. "There wasn't a damned thing wrong with that dress and you know it, but you embarrass your own daughter in front of your guests. You've taken a turn, old friend, and I don't know what it is."

George, holding himself erect on the edge of his chair, averts his face. "The party is barely underway," he says defiantly, "and already you've all turned on me. Blame George!

He's always the villain. Listen! If any of you understood the pressures I've been under, you wouldn't be so quick to judge!"

As if waking from a trance, Margaret flies across the room and seizes his sleeve.

"What's this?" he protests.

She drags him to his feet and out into the hall. He lets himself be dragged, and she whisks him around the corner, out of sight.

"What's this?" they all hear him say again.

She hisses, rapid-fire, "Do you want *her* to kill *her*self too?" She lowers her voice to an anguished plea. "George..." She pauses, then continues in a hardened, determined voice. "George, I'm leaving you!"

Richard can't imagine anyone in the room missed *that*.

Mrs. Moncure detaches herself from Richard's side. An ice cube snaps in somebody's glass.

Lucasta draws in her breath. "*Well!*"

"Pity so many of our beaches are posted now," says Toad, who's moved across to the window. "Don't suppose this one is though, unless that's a fisheries department notice on that tree down there. Of course poachers ignore the signs, don'tcha know."

No one responds. Billy plays with the ice in his drink.

"Tide at the full, don'tcha know," Toad goes on. "Or no, let's see, it was high at about five. Somewhere around there, don'tcha know."

Pris joins him at the window. She lays a hand on his arm. "Four-forty, according the *Chronicle*." she says. "I always read the tide tables. Everybody who lives here ought to. I have for as long as I can remember."

"What a *gorgeous* evening," says Lucasta, striking a grand pose on the sill of the French doors. "I think *I'll* take my mart' on the *veranda*. Margaret, dear heart, what's your mag*nifi*cent view *for* if no one *looks* at it?" She flares her nostrils, "*Smell* that air."

"Lucasta's having a hot flash," says Bea.

"Wind from the southwest, don'tcha know," Toad says, on his way out. Everyone follows.

In the hall doorway, Mrs. Moncure stands like a statue, looking silently on.

$$\text{ʂ} \quad \text{ʂ} \quad \text{ʂ}$$

Mrs. Moncure surveys the dining room table. Her hands flutter as she stands behind the chair where she was meant to sit. Abruptly she picks up her place card, lays it on her plate, gathers her napkin and silverware, and takes it all to the sideboard.

Flora looks up from the assembly line of cups of jellied madrilene, garnished with sour cream and caviar. She squints at Mrs. Moncure, who stands blocking the open doorway.

Mrs. Moncure speaks past Flora, to Richard. "Robin, the young have much to teach us. I shall not sit down at the table either. I'll go up to my Little Eyrie, change into something comfortable, and spend my evening there. Perhaps I could take a tray with me?"

Her "Little Eyrie" is the servant's room she's made her own. Flora rolls her eyes, reaches for a tray, flips a mat onto it, and adds a water glass.

"Some of your paté would be nice, Robin. Perhaps a cup of that delicious jellied madrilene. Mr. Moncure and I called our beautiful home our Eyrie, you know." The old lady makes another of her hand motions: she reaches up, as though for something on a shelf at eye level, and pinches the air.

Richard has never heard her address Flora. Now it seems she has become aware of her.

"My dear, I have been thinking what name would be nice for you. Now it comes to me: Fiona, possibly you know it? English, I believe, or perhaps Scottish. Thank you, I can manage the tray. I prefer wine. Robin, please tell Mrs. Wollaston I shall dine in my room."

Mrs. Moncure's absence will make the night longer for Richard. He finds her fanciful musings and soft incessant voice soothing, like classical music playing quietly in the background.

Flora mutters under her breath, "*Fiona! Robin! Little Eyrie!*"

On his way back to the front of the house, Richard pokes a finger at Flora's cups of ruby-red jelly. "Diced cucumbers," he reminds her.

George has just come back in from the porch and is helping Pris and Lucasta to rammers from the sweating martini pitcher Richard left behind.

"Hello, Geroge," Bea says. "We were just talking about Margaret's aunt. What does she call you?"

"Oh, she calls me Giorgio, I think...no, that's you, Lucasta. She calls me Geordie. She's a real joker. Move over, Lucasta, make room for your Uncle Giorgio on that chair. I know what I'll do, I'll sit on your lap."

George looks roguishly at Bea. "Shall I sit on Lucasta's lap?"

Bea shrugs. "Feel free."

Margaret too has returned and stands with her back to the room, hands braced stiffly on the windowsill, staring out at the sea.

Richard wonders how, after the scene George made with Angie, the others can still gather around him as if nothing happened. All except Margaret, who, in her dejection, reminds Richard again of his own mother. She resigned herself to carrying on the illusion that all was well with her world.

"Mrs. Wollaston," Richard says, "Mrs. Moncure has asked to be excused." He isn't sure she's heard him.

Then she turns and her eyes swim into focus. "Mrs. Moncure's all right?"

"I believe so. Perhaps tired."

The sky beyond the sea has turned a darker shade of red. Framed against its splendor is the silhouette of the porch railing. Angie left the gate open.

"I'd better fasten the porch gate, Mrs. Wollaston," Richard says. "I'll do it now while I think of it."

"Yes, please do, Richard."

3

TEN O'CLOCK

It's ten p.m. The damp air in the kitchen has the distinctive scent of dishwashing. It's whorled with smoke from Flora's cigarettes. In the front of the house, the party is on life support. Where is Angie? Richard, washing the dishes, berates himself for missing his chance. *If only I'd followed her into the woods*, he thinks, *I could have told her how I feel.*

She suddenly appears, the swinging pantry doors giving away her entry.

Richard takes a plate from the old Garland stove's warming oven. "We saved this for you," he says, offering it to her.

She distractedly receives the plate, stares at it, sets it on the counter. "If I ever have kids, I won't treat them the way Dad treats me," she mutters.

Richard secretly admires her filmy Indian-cotton dress. It becomes her. It seems a small matter to have produced such a reaction in her father. Anyone but George Wollaston would realize what a long way his daughter has come from the drug-dealing tomboy she used to be. Her putting on a dress at all is progress, and she has given up drugs entirely.

Without warning, Angie seizes Richard's best carving knife and plunges it savagely into the thick slice of steak he's saved for her. "Did you see Mom's face in there, Richard? Did you, Flora? I can take it, but I'm not sure Mom can."

She slowly relaxes her grip as she lowers the handle of the knife, rotating the blade out of the meat. As if in a daze, she stares at it, turning it over in her hand. "Richard, I love you, you know that. You and I'd raise kids right, wouldn't we?" She gently sets the knife down next to the plate.

"Of course we would," he says.

"So Richard, marry me."

He turns to her. "You're kidding!"

"I'm not kidding."

"Then you're crazy. He'll disinherit you. You'll lose your fortune."

"Richard, these last few years there's been something explosive between us. We've flirted and toyed..."

"We were *joking*," Richard interrupts.

"Only because I was underage," says Angie. "You could have had me any time you wanted, but you were too much of a gentleman. Well, now I'm eighteen, Richaahd. Eighteen. Marry me."

"No," he says. "You'd be doing it for the wrong reason — revenge."

"Then I'll just go drive off a *cliff!*"

Richard can only stand there, stunned, as he watches her turn and storm out the back door. A vivid memory comes back to him, of a similar scene. A winter storm had him and his mother cooped up in the house with his father, who was in one of his belligerent moods. Richard was so full of rage, yet there was no recourse: the Old Man would just turn it right back on him, evoking hellfire and brimstone and all that. Richard ran out into the blizzard, determined to freeze to death, right then and there. *That'll show him*, he thought. It wasn't long, however, before he doubled back and huddled on the lee side of the house. He didn't *really* want to do himself in; and besides, he couldn't leave his mother alone with that *beast*. Too proud to go back in, he made a mad dash for the barn to spend a cold, itchy night in the hay.

Richard becomes aware that he's heard a loud vehicle out in the driveway. The noise is gone now, and he was so lost in his reverie that he's not really sure what it sounded like. Angie's Porsche has a throaty roar whereas Dermott's truck has a guttural sputter, but they're both at about the same volume. He's not sure it was Angie's, as expected.

"Well, Richard!" says Flora, taking the roasting pan from him. "This calls for a celebration. I'm going to stay and help you finish up, as my little wedding present."

"No, no, you go home," he says. Events seem to be spinning out of control. He feels dizzy. "Did I hear Dermott's truck just now?"

"I *doubt* it."

Soon enough Flora's burley, flat-topped, red-faced husband will slouch into the kitchen. "How many drunks did you cater for tonight?" he'll ask with a slur of his own. Flora, with an air of the greatest relief, will snatch up her old cardigan. With her first smile of the evening, she'll tell Richard "good night."

"I *did* hear the truck," Richard insists.

She gives the pan a swipe. "After I finish this, I'm going to mop the floor."

"Have you had a fight with Dermott?"

"Me? Fight with Dermott?" She abruptly makes a quick departure with a reproving look and a parting crack: "No white mint. Tsk!" The pantry door slaps shut behind her.

If Flora wants to keep Dermott waiting, Richard decides, let her. Except for Angie's untouched dinner, his work is almost done. He prefers to do the final tidying up himself.

A warm wind has sprung up, lifting the kitchen curtains. It brings a faint thumping sound from the front of the house. George's stereo is playing the old stuff — "Sweet Georgia Brown" and "Crazy Rhythm." It's Lester Lanin's dry beat, calculated to make the listener dance an unvarying mechanical step with pumping elbows. Next will come "Just One of Those Things" and "You'd Be So Nice to Come Home To"... Richard knows the list; he's heard it so many times. Lucasta has them all dancing by now probably, or at least George and Toad will dance.

Richard packs up some of his gear and carries it out to his car. He finds the Subaru near the garage where Angie — his girl, his future wife...imagine that! — parked it. *Am I dreaming?* he wonders. He sees Dermott's truck parked in the usual spot by the old garage at the edge of the woods.

"Dermott *is* out there," he tells Flora when he gets back to the kitchen.

The buzzer sounds in the electric box above the sink, and a card marked "LIBRARY" clicks into place. Richard sheds his apron.

"They want ice in the library," he says. He trusts that when he returns he'll find Flora gone. He certainly hopes so.

ᔕ ᔕ ᔕ

In the library, Lucasta performs some kind of dance. At a safe distance, in the big wing chairs, George, Billy, and Toad watch with the enthusiasm of a row of seagulls.

Lucasta chants, "The ladies are lonely..." She exclaims, "Phew! Where do you get your cheap cigars, Giorgio darling? ...Time to join the ladies!" She shimmies across the room, picks Toad, and hauls him to his feet. "The music's playing, the girls are lonely," she reminds him. "This is a party, not a wake!" She waves a finger over Toad's shoulder at Richard. "Ice, Richard, ice; chop chop." Lucasta stops to turn her empty glass over to Richard. She takes Toad's glass from his hand and sets it on the tray too.

"Hey, Lucasta, calm down. I didn't finish that."

"Time for a refill," she says.

Not even Lucasta can bring this party to life. "In a Mountain Greenery" plays, then "Something's Gotta Give." When "Volare" comes on, she lays a flushed cheek against Toad's and propels him with her out the door, across the hall, and into the living room.

In the living room, Margaret stares out the window. Bea and Pris sit apart. As Lucasta drags Toad sweating down the center of the room, Bea hastily withdraws her gold-kid-shod feet.

"Time to go home," Bea says.

Lucasta lets Toad go. It takes time for the urge to ripen in her; she begins her skit, which she often performs at parties. She struts through the room, twirling a cane as she sings in an old-time vaudeville voice, "'Twas a dark and stormy night, the night I ran away, I'll never fergit it till my dyin' day. 'Twas a dark and stormy night..." Richard has never heard her get past this opening line.

Bea snatches the cane away.

Not Lucasta's song nor the sight of the moon's path on the sea; not the heady scents of the Maine coast in late summer, nor even a fresh pitcher of stingers can resurrect George's party. Margaret turns off the stereo. Enid slips away into the woods. Toad raises a fuss about Lucasta having seen something out one of the front hall windows.

"What did you see?" he pleads, but she floats out the door clutching her shell-beaded purse to her red silk bosom. She has to uncork the driveway so Billy can begin his half-hour-long drive home to Mountpeace.

Toad and Les Girls are going to ride with Bea in her Mercedes. At the last minute, Bea reports a lost earring; there's a free-for-all turning out of sofa and chair cushions. On their halting way out, the trio stands docilely swaying by the open front door while Richard searches with a flashlight along the baseboard. The evening air pours in through the screen door. Outside, in the driveway's turn-around, George bellows in a joyful, off-key voice, "The tree, the tree, the tree! Lucasta hit the tree. Hi, ho my Derry oh, Lucasta hit the tree!"

They are all too drunk to wonder how the accident happened or what, if anything, came of it. Accidents like this aren't rare. Lucasta backs away from the tree, then roars off into the darkness. They hear the rumble of loose gravel as she swerves off the road more than once.

"Who's driving?" asks Toad.

"I am. My car." Bea holds up her key.

Pris snatches it from her hand. "You've had *much* too much to drink, Bea dearie. *I'm* driving," she says with a hiccup.

Richard hears giggles, car doors slamming, the rasp of an ignition, a roar, and a thump: Pris, at the wheel of Bea's Mercedes, has given the beech tree a fresh wound. Silence follows. He heaves the heavy old library chairs into place and wipes ashes from the tabletops. He hopes Pris will start the car up again, that he won't be asked to help. He leaves ice in the bar in the likely event that George decides to make himself a nightcap.

Still no sounds from the driveway.

Are Toad and Les Girls on their way in for another round of drinks? Richard hopes not. Peeking out the front windows, he sees the Mercedes nose to nose with the tree. Pris, behind the wheel, has one side of her kindly aristo-cratic face mashed, asleep, into the leather backrest. Bea, slumped in the passenger seat, is barely visible over the dashboard. Is that Toad with his head under the hood and George on his way to the house for some tools? The hall clock chimes four faltering strokes: no one has wound it. Richard checks his watch. It's eleven forty-five, much earlier than these parties usually wind down.

Richard stands for a moment in the living room, surveying the scene. An unfinished glass sweats on the mantel, an ashtray overflows, a stemmed glass is sticky with mint and cognac. He absently collects these, his eyes on the moonlit lawn beyond the porch. Over the wind in the trees, he hears the Mercedes roar away as if it were full of teenagers.

He hears Margaret say, "Please go to bed, Aunt Beth."

"I beg you, Mellicent," Mrs. Moncure answers. "Oh my dear, I do *beg* you. Divorce is so...superfluous. These things *can* be worked out."

The screen door slams, the hall lights go out, flash on, then off again. It's George, fooling with the switch. "Lost!" he cries. The lights come on. "Found!" he joyfully shouts. He sings, "Prissy hit the tree, Prissy hit the tree, hi ho my Derry oh, Prissy hit the tree!"

George is on the move again, and Richard sees him tack abruptly.

"Where *is* everybody?" George says. He peers into a doorway and turns away. Then he snaps his head back for a second look, like a comedian's delayed reaction. Supporting himself with one hand on the doorframe, he says scornfully, "Party sure as hell isn't in *there*." On he comes, on a slant. "Must be *somebody* friendly around here. My wife and her aunt..." With an airy wave, he dismisses Margaret and Mrs. Moncure. "Oh there you are, Richard, old man. You know where my friends are?"

Richard thinks, *You have no friends, Mr. Wollaston.* He steadies his tray. "Everyone's gone home, Mr. Wollaston."

"Home?" George repeats, incredulous. "It's barely midnight. The party should just be getting... Ah, what's the use? She's turned them all against me. Look at that sky, Richard old man. What a night. How about bringing me a nightcap on the porch?" George goes out, pushing the screen door wide open. It slams shut behind him.

"Just go on up to bed, Aunt Beth, please," Margaret says. Her tense figure emerges from a doorway. The old lady follows, her back straight as a ramrod. In the dim light of the hallway sconces, Margaret's face looks drained. Mrs. Moncure looks shocked. Richard watches her lift a hand to her cheek. He looks away for a moment, then they're gone.

§ § §

Delivering George's nightcap, Richard finds his employer sunken deeply among the cushions of the porch's big wicker sofa. A glass ashtray tilts on the sofa's arm. Moonlight reaches in under the porch roof, illuminating the white handrail around the perimeter like a picture frame.

George takes the glass from Richard's tray and says, "Richard, I want to ask you something. I know I can count on you. Was I out of order tonight?"

More than anything, Richard wants the night to be over. Once again he sees Crawford's pale indoor face and hears the old man's dry voice: "Whatever you do, never get drawn into their personal lives in any way. You hear me? In *any* way."

"Richard, a man in your line of work," said George one night last summer, "knows about drinking."

It was late in the evening, and Richard was packing up his gear in the kitchen. George set his glass of scotch down among Richard's carving knives on the table, pulled out a chair, and sat. "Sit down, Richard old man. I want to talk to you man to man".

Richard felt oppressed, finding himself cornered so near the end of his day. He wiped his hands on his apron.

George eyed him across the table. "Do you think I drink too much?"

"It's not for me to say, Mr. Wollaston," Richard said.

"Don't give me weasel words," said George, with a hint of a wavering stutter in his speech. "You know me, I know you. You and I are talking man to man here. Pour yourself a drink. Come on, a man needs a drink for a serious talk. This is strictly *entre nous*. How long have I known you? Ten years? I know you as a man I can depend on. Mrs. Wollaston has been after me: she says I drink too much. She says I never used to show it, but now I do. Is she right? Tell me frankly." George went on, as though he hadn't yet made his point. "This is just between you and me. Whatever you say I won't hold it against you. I realize a man in your line of work sees things. I know you're a sensible fellow. Do me a favor and give me your opinion on this. Go on, fix yourself something. I know all you guys drink. You know where the bottles are. Make yourself something."

"I'd rather not, Mr. Wollaston."

"Well, I can't force a man to do something he doesn't want to. Now, man to man, is Mrs. Wollaston right?"

Richard clearly saw Crawford's ghost behind George's chair, his mouth compressed, disapproving, signaling, *Don't be a fool.* But Richard thought it possible he could do George a favor. George had asked a serious question. Clearly he was appealing for help. And besides, Crawford was dead.

Richard said reluctantly, "You do drink quite a lot, Mr. Wollaston."

"But not a problem, eh?" said George, standing up. He smacked his flat belly. "I told her that. I told her I keep in shape. I told her I eat. I said if I had a problem with booze, I wouldn't eat, would I?"

That sounded far-fetched to Richard. However, same as his father, George would probably convince himself of anything to defend his tenuous position.

"I knew I could depend on you, Richard."

Now Richard is in the same bind again, only he's not as sympathetic as he was before.

"Was I out of order in there before dinner?" George asks. "I mean with Angie?"

Richard lies, "I don't remember anything untoward, Mr. Wollaston."

George gives him an approving look. "I knew I could depend on you," he says. "A man always knows who his real friends are."

4

GEORGE ON THE PORCH

It occurs to George that he's pretty high up here on the porch. Pretty good drop to the lawn. He calls out, "Hey, Margaret, I'm still out here!" Wind's blowing; probably she can't hear. He rattles the doorknob and bangs on the glass. Locked up like a bank. No point in trying to see in. As dark in there as the inside of his pocket. Just the reflection of his face in the glass. Don't they know he's out here? Who locked the goddamn door? This isn't New York; this isn't some goddamn ghetto. He'll smash in the glass. No. Costs too much to fix. He isn't a man to vandalize his own house.

The only way is down those steps... He's sober enough to know he's drunk, and that would be dangerous.

Something's amiss. The gate across the top of the steps: it's open. "The drunk gate" she calls it. Not a nice thing to say. When he and his brother were kids, there wasn't a gate. They put mattresses down there and jumped off. There aren't any mattresses down there now. He's no kid.

Good sofa here, though; long enough for a tall man. Warm night, night made for sleeping on porches.

Who was with him just now? Freshened his drink? If so, where's his glass?

Maybe Margaret has a point. Maybe his brain *is* going, shrinking to the size of an olive in one of his damn martinis, as she says. She has a fine way of expressing herself. She says lots of things these days she never said before. A man's wife ought to stick by her husband. She ought not to pick on him just because he makes a few mistakes. She goes too far... Wants him to quit drinking! How's that for unreasonable? Everybody knows he drinks. He's never made a secret of it. Never falls down. Never mixes up his speech. He's got the stamina of a horse. What's the fuss?

About his brain, he can remember a few things. Tonight, a party, his idea; he remembers that. Not much of a party, just a few old friends. Did he do something he shouldn't have done? Something he shouldn't have said to Angie? Did Margaret threaten to leave him tonight? She'd never leave him... May threaten but wouldn't act...or was that a dream?

He wonders if anybody is looking for him. Doesn't anybody miss him? He'd miss Margaret if *she* were locked out on the porch. Maybe *her* brains also need looking into.

She's gone upstairs: light's shining on the elm...her window just above this end of the porch. Light on out back too...probably Richard washing up. Let's see: used to be a bell on this porch. You rang it and they heard it in the kitchen. Where's the bell now? Good old Richard, he never nags a man. Probably likes a snort himself. All those guys do. Oops, table here. Ouch! Where's that goddamn bell?

ॐ ॐ ॐ

That time she had him hauled off to the emergency room, some nut doctor tried to sign him into detox. That's how she gets when she wants something. She took him to one of her meetings.

Woman with a pointer, about fifteen people, the jargon-words come back to him. "Enabler...dependent... hero..." He scorns their made-up language. Pointer woman was as sure of herself as an old-time preacher.

"Stand on that chair, George," she said.

Where does she come off first-naming me? he thought, indignant.

"Margaret, you stand in front of George. Angie, you stand beside Margaret." Picked a kid to play their son Tony. Tony! This pointer woman really knew where the sore spots are. George would never admit it, but Tony's death is the biggest regret of his life.

"Your beer," the woman said, handing George an imaginary glass.

"I don't drink beer," he told her.

"What do you drink then?"

"Gin," he said testily.

"All right, George, your gin's in that corner. Pretend you see it, and don't take your eyes off it. Stand on that

chair... Put your hands on your wife's shoulders... Come
on. If you don't you'll lose your balance."

Very clever: nobody could stand on a chair and concentrate on something on the other side of a room and
keep his balance. He felt Margaret's shoulders tighten as
he gripped them. Angie pressed against her. He was a good
size for them.

George concentrated so hard on his gin, he couldn't see
the kid capering about. Tony was the "hero," as the woman
called him.

"Now, do you all see what's happening here?"

All in attendance nodded. Scattered responses:

"Oh yes."

"Indeed."

"Very enlightening."

"Ridiculous," George snapped. "I don't see anything."

"Well, George" the woman said, "Tony's role is to
take your wife's and your daughter's minds off holding you up." She coolly waved her pointer. She was in
charge. George thinks a good stiff snort would've done
her good.

"Relax," the woman told George, "you can come down
now. Margaret and Angie, you sit over there. Have the rest
of you any comments you'd like to make on Margaret-and-
George-and-Angie's family sculpture?"

Family sculpture! George burst out laughing.

An old guy stood up. George recognized him from
around town. "You might think this is funny, George," the
old guy said, "but you didn't realize that two little women

like Margaret and Angie could hold up a big guy like you, did you?"

"It's all so transparent!" George bellowed. "It's all a setup to trick me! An inside look at my life! And Margaret, you going along with it! Humbling yourself! Humiliating me! Where's your pride? Your common sense? If my mother were alive, she'd yank me out of here. And you, and Angie too. My mother would give us all what for."

Mother... George must have been six, listening outside her bedroom door. She was whispering, weeping. He was scared. His old man was pleading about something. What was that about? The old man never gave up drinking, so that couldn't have been it. Could it? Was there something he's missing?

Since Tony's death, Margaret's never been the same. Overnight a difference. Blames Tony's death on my drinking. Something knocks a woman like her off balance, then she's fair game for any nut woman waving a pointer.

๑ ๑ ๑

Clock chiming inside the house. House full of clocks. His father taught him to wind the clocks. Taught him to make a proper martini. "Don't bruise the gin," his old man said. If no French vermouth, then Italian; if no vermouth, the smallest drop of Scotch.

Don't they know I'm out here? They don't care. All turned against me. My own children, my own wife.

Where am I? Oh yes, on the porch. Locked out of my own house, middle of the night. Damn thirsty. Where's my glass?

What a moon! Fellow on a boat, night like this, would have porpoises cavorting under the bow, all lit up with the phosphorescence in the water, warm air blowing off the land. Best thing in Maine, a night of southwest wind.

Moon in the southeast now. Pretty late. Maybe shouldn't have had that last drink. I might try holding the rail and going down the steps bass ackwards, like an old sailor going down a ship's ladder. Well, I'll just rest here a minute. Unfortunately I'm sobering up.

All the doctors ever tell a man is double talk. How much are you drinking, George? I have a cocktail before dinner for God's sake, Doc, what about you? I like a drink now and then, Doc, it's a civilized way to live.

"Mr. Wollaston?"

That's a real voice. "Tiger!" George shouts.

"Mr. Wollaston, is everything all right?"

"Well, not exactly, Tiger." But he realizes that most of his words scatter in the rising wind.

Voice very formal: "Don't call me 'Tiger,' Mr. Wollaston. I'm Officer Perham." Glint of a badge, sheen of leather: cop now. James Perham. Native kid. Cop. Never Tiger again.

George feels a rush of shame. He has things to account for. "Forgive me, Tiger!"

Still, the problem hasn't changed; he has to get off the porch in one piece. Patch things up with Angie. She'll help him. He creeps to the edge of the porch and squints down. Wind's blowing like stink.

"Go back inside there, Mr. Wollaston."

The moon sails out from behind the clouds and George sees James. Except for the uniform, no different from when George first laid eyes on him, a little trespasser on the beach. What would have been wrong with having a kid like that for a son-in-law? Ah, George went too far there too. He's done plenty he isn't proud of.

Something funny about this night. Moon's little more than a quarter - but almost as bright as full - shining out suddenly then hiding; wind rushing in the trees, roaring like a locomotive.

Tiger saying something, wind drowning him out. "Steps... Mr... Dangerous... Good night..." The wind whips his voice away, then he's gone.

Something more did Tiger say? "Hell of an anniversary." Did Tiger say that?

The lawn so white! The ocean white, sky white, then clouds blot it all out.

All right then, George old man, on your own. Just through this gate. One step at a time, same as the woman with the pointer said. Turn around, face in, grab on to the railing. Up to you, nobody here to help.

His predicament strikes him as funny. Fellow with a camera could get a good one. Come on, George old man, just down the first step. But the first step is a bastard.

One. Two. Three... Slip, bumpity-thump, crack!

Gosh, that was a close one: almost went overboard. Stand up and stretch, work the kinks out. Oop, loosing my balance here... Quick, better shove off so I don't hit any more of these damn steps...

Flying!

Crack, ka-thump; flash like fireworks going off. Good Christ. Something broken here - not funny...

5

IN THE SILENT HOUSE

At the back of the house, Richard works to finish up as quickly as possible. He unhooks and raises the lid of the wooden trash bin, drops in the slick plastic sack, lowers the lid back down, and hooks the catch against raccoons. Above him is Mrs. Moncure's lighted window. The shadow, projected onto its drawn shade, shows her sitting at her table. The shade blows in on the breeze, and the shadow gives a start. Richard imagines Mrs. Moncure up there, comforting herself after the unpleasant scene in the living room.

He's seen her "Little Eyrie." One night he went up to use the maids' toilet. He'd believed that part of the house to be empty, so he was surprised to find one of the rooms occupied. Greeting cards were scotch-taped everywhere on the walls and woodwork. There were stickers of bluebirds and canaries and thatched cottages. A collection of perfume bottles and china figurines stood around a few paperback novels. He remembers *Wuthering Heights* and *Rebecca*.

Not much moonlight gets through this dense grove of maples at the back end of the house. Richard can make out forms though. He sees that there's still a pickup out by the old garage where Dermott parks when he comes to get Flora. They're long gone, he figures, so it must be one of Angie's friends. A speck of light shows on the windshield of the truck — a reflection, it appears, of Enid Wollaston's driveway lights winking through the swaying spruce branches.

Flora's gone. She's cleaned up all but Angie's plate with its big slab of steak, still oozing blood from its wound. Richard has the place to himself. He brought a bottle of George's Armagnac from the library on his last trip. He lifts it from under the sink and pours himself a shot. One of Crawford's rules was no drinking on the job ("Do as I say, not as I do," the old sinner said slyly, giving Richard an arch look). His work is done. Margaret's kitchen has the orderly look of which he approves. He's given her money's worth — made the paté himself, baked the small crackers to go with it, made the rolls — and she took the trouble to thank him.

"Angie has her key," she said. "You can lock up."

"What about Mr. Wollaston?" Richard asked her. "Is there something more I can do for him?"

"I think not," she answered. The kitchen fixtures' unforgiving light showed lines between her brows, giving her pleasant features a grim expression.

Richard hopes Margaret and Angie can find an opportunity to console each other.

"Do the best you can, even if you despise them" was another of Crawford's precepts. "Be the first to arrive and the last to go. Wash the Minton by hand even if only a dozen plates are left and half of those are chipped and the gold luster's worn off. If you break one, offer to pay. They'll never let you. These people may be tight with their money, but if they think you're worth it, they'll pay. Never let them get chummy. If one says, 'Call me by my first name,' don't be tempted — some will try it when they're plastered. Watch your step with Bea Bassett."

Richard wonders at the memory of Crawford's pallid, sardonic, indoor face and the odor of dry cleaning on his black coat. Why is the old man so much in his thoughts tonight? Crawford came close to being a father-like figure to Richard. He's been dead four years.

Warming the balloon glass in his cupped palms, feeling the brandy warm his gut, Richard lifts his face to the soft wind pouring through the open window. Mrs. Moncure's message for the night was "things are tough all over."

ᔆ ᔆ ᔆ

Like a clip of an old film, Richard sees a scene from his life as a boy of nine at the parsonage in Deep River. Frost flowers spread across the windowpanes and a lilac branch ticks against the glass, during a bitter maritime April.

"Rats deserting the ship, is it?" Richard's father, the Reverend Andrew Grassie, wore the same air of amused expectation as George Wollaston. "For better, for worse, in sickness, in health, all that means nothing then?" He laughed, the same way George laughs, and quoted Robert Burns:

> *"Oh ye who are sae guid yoursel,*
> *Sae pious and sae holy,*
> *Ye've naught to do but mark and tell*
> *Your neighbor's faults and folly."*

With this, he drew a bottle from his pocket and presented it with a bow to Richard's mother, Clara.

> *"Ye high, exalted, virtuous Dame,*
> *Tied up in godly laces,*
> *Before ye give poor Frailty names,*
> *Suppose a change o' cases."*

Clara ignored Andrew, swaying in the doorway, offering up his treasure. With the back of a floury wrist, she pushed at her sandy hair slipping from its green ribbon. She turned over her bread dough and slapped it hard on the board. She looked at Richard and said, "Soon it'll be time to take off the storm sashes, Richard, sweetheart."

Andrew never gave up a bottle without leaving an unopened twin in the cupboard or behind the boots or behind the books in his study.

One evening Richard was struggling to please Clara by making additional space for the storm sashes in the shed. He sniffed an odd odor; hot metal, as it turned out, and smoldering cloth, near the point of catching fire. Smoke, thin as a hair, curled from under the door of his father's study. The next thing he remembers is seeing his father's heavy frame, collapsed facedown on his desk. His small mother was trying to lift the body.

Was it the heat that killed him or fumes accumulated from the sheet-iron woodstove in the small, closed room? A drinker's damaged heart? In that part of Canada, no one thought to do autopsies, not in those days. Mired in the desk's blistered varnish, smashed under Andrew's flushed cheek, his notebook lay open. It was not his notes for the week's sermon he'd been working on but a slanting, wobbly line from Robert Burns, smudged to near illegibility:

"Last night the gypsies came to our house and wow but they sang sweetly."

ဪ ဪ ဪ

Richard called his father "Andrew." The more familiar "Dad" never seemed right to him since he was little. He continues to be haunted by imaginary scenes in which he stood up to Andrew. He never had the courage to put any one of them into action.

George's son, Tony, stood up to his father in a way that Richard admires. It was another time when Richard overheard, by way of the heat ducts, a conversation at the other end of the house. Richard was in the pantry, polishing silverware, and Tony and George were in the study. The tinkle of ice and the chink of glassware were what got his attention. He's always amazed by how the sound carries so well. It's like the old voice tubes built in to some of these cottages, but this ductwork conveys nearly any ambient sound.

It was the summer Tony brought his girl, Nickie, home.

"I'm different from you, Dad," Richard heard Tony say. "I want different things out of life."

"That's *good*," George said in his loud voice, heavy with irony. "Because you'll never get anywhere among the people you grew up with if you saddle yourself with *that* girl. She'll be like an anchor around your neck." After a brief pause, George continued in a different sort of voice, bullying: "Then you'll *really* find out about a different sort of life...and don't turn to *me* for help." Silence for a few tense moments, then George's attack turned accusing, taunting: "You always did get yourself into trouble. *Now* who're you going to turn to? Answer me *that*! Go ahead! Just don't think anybody *else* is going to help you. You don't have any friends out there!"

Richard discovered he'd been holding his breath. It seemed that a long time passed before he heard another word. He stood petrified, as though his own father had just laid into him. He wanted to run the water to rinse the silver but desisted in case he'd miss something. He couldn't move anyway.

Tony finally said in a surprisingly calm voice, "Your word isn't everything, Dad. I *spit* on your world... Mom's too. She buys all this *crap*."

Richard felt a shock surge through his body like a lightning bolt. He was perfectly safe at the other end of the house from George and Tony. Yet he stood galvanized, his breath shallow, the blood hot in his ears.

After a brief pause: "Have it your way, Tone." Then George was bullying again: "Go ahead! You marry that girl, you'll never get a penny of my money. See how you like *that*!"

In the silence that followed, Richard slowly took up his polishing rag again. The fork he was working on had been rubbed clean. Like a man in a trance, he rubbed it again. The blood pounded in his head.

Quick footsteps rapped on the oak floors, echoing along the hall. The pantry door burst open, and Tony thrust his head in. At first, Richard thought it was George — the resemblance was so strong. "Where's Mom? Good-bye, Richard."

"Good-bye?" he asked stupidly.

"Good-bye," Tony said and shook Richard's hand. "I'm looking for Mom. Nickie and I are shoving off."

Nickie appeared in the doorway. "Your dad'll feel different in the morning," she said timidly.

Tony replied in a vehemently bitter tone, "Yes, and hell will freeze over in the morning!"

Before Richard finished the forks, he heard Tony's Maserati out front. Through the open window he heard the voices of Margaret and Angie out there saying good-bye, but not a peep from George.

ᔈ ᔈ ᔈ

Richard's mouth puckers from the astringent aftertaste of George's Armagnac. He should be home in Horseshoe Cove. Tomorrow will be another crowded day of his busiest season. Three inches remain in the bottle. He corks it, washes and dries the glass, then carries both through the silent house to put them away in the library. The French doors of the living room frame a view of the water, out beyond the moonstruck lawn and fitfully thrashing trees. His caterer's eye detects a crumpled napkin by the doors. As he picks it up, it occurs to him that he's forgotten to bring in George's glass. These doors are kept locked, but while he's here...

He draws back the bolt. As he steps onto the porch, the wind, swirling around, sends the door banging shut behind him. No glass: Margaret must have picked it up. George, or the wind, has overturned a table. The drunk gate is open, swinging in the breeze. Richard rights the table and moves to close the gate. Something at the foot of the stairs catches his eye. It's Pris's sweater no doubt. She probably left it draped over the railing again, and the wind carried it off. Not his responsibility. Sliding the metal latch into place brings to mind his mother and the gate she had installed at the head of the staircase to keep Andrew from falling. He shakes out the sofa cushions, surveys the view once more, and walks around the porch, looking for anything out of place...

Whatever's lying at the foot of the stairs is too big for a sweater. What is it? Richard opens the gate and makes his way down the steep steps. As he does so, the moon soars out from behind the clouds to reveal George, lying there. What a strange position he lies in, arms flung out, head thrown back, as if in mid-flight he managed to turn himself around. One of his slippers has been thrown clear and lies apart in the moonlight.

Richard kneels and extends a hand. After a moment of frozen shock, he abruptly draws it back. George appears to be laughing. His last thought must have been wonderfully funny.

6

RICHARD UPSTAIRS

Richard finds himself at the top of the front stairs, in a part of George's house he's never seen. He's at the end of a broad, paneled hallway with pictures everywhere. Margaret's door must be the one with the bar of yellow light under it, since Mrs. Moncure's Little Eyrie is at the other end of the house.

He knocks, aware of the hot adrenaline in him and of a curious state of mind, as if his brain were paralyzed.

No answer. He knocks again.

"Yes?" she finally answers, faintly.

"It's Richard, Mrs. Wollaston." Should he open the door?

"Yes?" comes her voice again. In a panic he turns the knob. She is sitting up in bed, wearing some kind of white shawl or sweater and earphones. She reaches across to the nightstand and clicks off a small tape player.

"Something's happened," he begins and then falters. "Something's happened... Mrs. Wollaston, I... We ought to call the police."

Her eyes look enormous. She tugs the shawl to her throat. She, with her bedside light, is at the center of an island of brightness. In the surrounding gloom, he sees a dressing table, a desk and chairs, a chaise longue, and an open suitcase on a luggage stand at the foot of the bed.

"Police?" she echoes and gestures toward the telephone as if to say, *You do it.*

As Richard dials, he sees again his father's face crushed against the crumpled, inky page. He feels with his whole body the furnace-like heat of that room, close to combustion.

An enthusiastic young voice answers. Richard gives Margaret's name and, since the dispatcher sounds new to the job, he spells it and gives directions to the house.

ᔕ ᔕ ᔕ

The police car's flashing blue light catches Richard full in the face, blinding him. He puts up a hand to shield his eyes and hears a siren in the distance. The pulsing light, combined with the intermittent moonlight, creates an eerie, surreal effect.

He recognizes the two policemen who jump out of the car. The older man, Webber, wears lieutenant's bars; and James Perham is Angie's friend, the one George called "Tiger." Richard waves them around the house. As they set off, Webber turns back to bellow, "Move that little foreign car for us, will you?"

The Porsche reeks of mechanics' tinned soap and greasy rags. Richard can make out a jumble of tools in the passenger foot-well and, on the seat, a sand dollar. Angie has left the keys in the ignition, but in the haste of his panic he finds the car impossible to start. The ambulance has arrived. He abandons his assignment.

"That way," he calls to the driver, pointing.

Someone has turned on the floodlights, up under the eaves on the sea side of the house. Richard sees James, Webber, and Margaret, standing in a huddle, looking down at George's body. High above stands Mrs. Moncure, small and straight-backed, at the porch railing with her hands folded at her waist, looking down. She is wearing a white wrapper that flutters in the wind.

"Who's that?" the lieutenant whispers.

"Mrs. Wollaston's aunt," James whispers back.

"Don't touch anything up there, missus," Webber calls to her.

Like a ghost in her gauzy, floating Indian print dress, Angie materializes out of the darkness and joins her mother.

Within minutes the ambulance crewmen's postures tell the story. From where they crouch, they glance up at Margaret, then quickly at Angie, then at the policemen. In an effort to dispel the tension of the moment, one murmurs in a deep local accent, "Don't the sea smell strong down here, though."

The sweet scent of trampled grass fills the air, and Richard smells the sea — rather the shore at low tide. His thoughts turn to George's glass. Did he put away the Armagnac? He'd rather Margaret's cleaning woman not find it in the morning.

§ § §

Police Chief Eliot is a tall, good-looking man at fifty. He climbs out of his truck to confront something he has dreaded much of his life.

"One of them handrails is loose," the lieutenant says in greeting, "and the fifth tread from the top is broke. James called Wilcox for you." The lieutenant pauses, glances in Richard's direction, and adds, "Fellow over there says there was a party."

Chief Eliot stares at the treacherous flight of steps and at George's body splayed on the grass below it. He's reminded of the time he was called over here in the middle of the night last summer. George had fallen over the stairway banister of the upstairs hall. His fall was broken when his shoulder landed on an oak stair tread two or three steps from the bottom. It cracked the tread and broke the shoulder. It must have been quite a crash, but Margaret slept right through it. George somehow got himself to the phone to call the police...and complained of a burglar in the house. That was the time Anne Frasier, of the substance abuse department at the hospital, explained to Margaret what she was up against.

The strap of George's watchband has pulled out of its buckle. His tie is loosened, his collar open. These last he did himself, Chief Eliot reasons: the night is warm. The watchband could have caught on something as he fell.

Margaret says, "Talk about spoiling a party!"

Chief Eliot is hardly surprised that his one-time friend should come to such an end, but her words give him a jolt.

He's heard of sudden widows saying a lot of things, but this hits a nerve.

"Yeah! Yeah!" exclaims Angie, thrusting her fist triumphantly into the air. He wonders if she's high.

These days, except for what Chief Eliot hears in town and the little his nephew James confides in him, he isn't up on the Wollastons' news. Now and again one of his men brought George up for speeding or nailed one of Angie's druggie friends, but Chief Eliot has kept his distance. He is struck by the scene: the night, the hour, the house, the moon, and here lies his estranged old friend George, dead. He never knew how it would happen; he just knew it would.

🌀 🌀 🌀

Chief Eliot knows George's house. He can taste the syrupy green jam the Wollastons' cooks made years ago from the hairy fruit on that vine under the porch. It used to be kept pruned back, but now it runs amok all the way up and onto the roof.

His muscles still feel the weight of that stone bench, grandly facing the sea on one side of the high porch steps. His fingers remember the bench's weathered surface. For a prank, he and George and George's brother Lyle enlisted some friends to help move the thing. Somehow they got a skid under it and, with ropes and a tremendous amount of sweat, dragged it to the foot of the lawn, gouging a furrow a hundred yards long in George's father's bent-grass turf. They levered it off the bank onto the beach. There it settled, deeper with every tide, up to its gargoyle-carved seat. George's father spent a fortune on a barge and crane to hoist it out. Eliot was scared, but George just laughed, and Lyle lied himself out of the whole thing. Old Mr. Wollaston, unpredictable as the weather (especially when he'd had a few, as usual) did nothing to punish either one. Chief Eliot has not forgotten the hiding he got at home, though, for that stunt.

ஞ ஞ ஞ

Richard stands apart from the other men, away from Margaret and Angie, and from the old lady in the fussy white bathrobe up on the porch. Chief Eliot studies Richard's tired face, then beckons to him.

There's liquor on his breath. It has been Chief Eliot's impression that Richard always works sober. A Canadian, he showed up in French Haven one summer in the '70s and found work at the swimming club. Listening to Richard's account of the evening, Chief Eliot knows he could have told the story himself. No part of the evening holds any surprise. George was drinking — nothing new there. He had a last drink on the porch, nothing unusual in that either. He had the constitution of a horse, could really sock the stuff away. Then he fell; no surprise, considering he was taken to the hospital for the same fall a couple of years ago. This time, though, he broke his neck.

Richard has finished speaking. Chief Eliot missed his last words — odd for so experienced a policeman. He knows

Richard only slightly. He wonders what time he usually goes home. Chief Eliot imagines the sequel here. Since the State of Maine no longer routinely holds inquests, Wilcox will rule it an unattended accidental death, and Margaret and Angie will go on as before... No, they'll be in better shape. That is clear enough from what they said and from how they look now — side by side, each with an arm around the other. Neither of them looks grief-stricken.

For a man who wrote off George Wollaston, Chief Eliot is unprepared for his own reaction. He's nearly choked up with overpowering, stifling sadness. He had, after all, such a friendly, almost brotherly relationship with George, years ago.

Up on the porch, the old lady makes some motion or other. Webber will have the word on her; Chief Eliot's lieutenant is nothing if not thorough. Eliot sighs and turns back to Richard.

"Come by in the morning," he tells him. "We'll need a statement for the record."

7

AFTER MIDNIGHT

Enid, making her way home from George's house for the second time tonight, is halfway through the strip of woods between the two houses when she hears the police arrive. *Ah*, she thinks, *Angie*. Supposedly on the straight and narrow these days...fat chance. Enid knows pot smoke when she smells it: she noticed it on the boy George hired, when she met him in the driveway this afternoon. Bringing drugs to Angie, she supposes.

She got home from the party, made herself comfortable, and watched part of an old movie before she realized she'd left her purse at George's.

She's glad she went back. The purse lay where she dropped it in George's driveway, not far from the front door. By morning, cars would have mashed it into the gravel. A pebble has lodged inside her slipper. She stoops to feel around for it with a forefinger.

She forges on, back toward Outer Mongolia. Who could have been mean enough to give a nice house such a nickname? She slips occasionally in the loose spruce duff. Poor George. One child's gone, the other's out of control, and his wife is clearly no help to him; she also looks her age. What an awful scene back there at dinner, when all conversation ended in the same quelled embarrassment! Enid still feels the warmth of George's mouth on hers. Speak of embarrassment! She hears another siren. Her own porch lights beckon.

ଽ ଽ ଽ

Richard is going out to pack the rest of his gear into the Subaru. As he makes his way toward the back door, he hears the abrupt rumble and sputter of an old vehicle starting up. It sounds a bit like Dermott's cacophonous old heap, but then quiets down to a low, thumping idle. He goes out the door to find, sure enough, the truck he saw earlier. The tempo and volume pick up slightly, and the truck rolls slowly out into the driveway, lights off. That's just like some of Angie's old friends, creeping around on the sly...as best they can, anyway, with a bad muffler. He hoped she had shed them.

ଽ ଽ ଽ

Angie stares down at her father's body. He was laughing. Everything was a joke to him, all the way.

When she was little, she and Tony loved to watch *Batman*. Their father, drink in hand, often sauntered into the room, stood a moment watching the TV, then roared with laughter. He shouted, "Bam! Zap! Pow! Kaboom!" reciting the exclamations from the cartoons that started the show. The children made efforts to hear the dialogue, but that only egged him on; asking him to stop just made it worse.

He turned to throw a conspiratorial look at Angie and Tony, as though they wanted to join in making malicious fun of their own joy. Seeming to revel in their oppressed expressions, he bellowed out the Batman theme song: "Dada dada dada dada da: *Batman*..." With a glint in his eye, he carried on in defiance of the children's discomfort. They couldn't hear what the Riddler, the Joker, or any other character had to say. Sometimes he carried on until they were reduced to tears.

To George it was merely teasing, just a lot of fun. To Angie and Tony it was entirely serious, as far as they could tell. Their father, after all, had the voice of authority, had their trust...until he began to attack them. Laughter was his weapon, laced with irony and ridicule. He used his weapons thoughtlessly and thoroughly, seemingly unaware that the kids were too young to understand or defend themselves. George especially loved to tease Tony... Teased him right to death, as it turned out.

Margaret, looking down at George's body, feels short of breath. Her heart drums in her chest, and she feels lightheaded. She loved George! She did! With all her heart she loved the man he'd been, such a long time ago.

The lieutenant, or whatever he is, cranes his neck around and studies her.

Mrs. Moncure looks on. Poor Geordie, such a fine, educated man, a gentleman born but lately so changed. A tease, he always enjoyed himself, but he was never cruel, not at first anyway. She'd liked him so much. It was such a terrible thing for that nice Robin to have to find him like that, to have the sad duty of calling Mellicent. Mrs. Moncure knows what unpleasantness is. She understands what Robin must be feeling. She knows what Mellicent and Andrea are experiencing too, down there arm in arm. The older policeman looks up and catches Mrs. Moncure's eye. She nods to him, civilly.

ゐ ゐ ゐ

Chief Eliot retires to his little house behind the post office. He goes right to the bedroom, hangs his baton, belt, and holster on a chair, then sits to untie his shoes. The low-ceilinged room is stuffy. The wind, which roisters in the trees along the shore and has poured over the town all night, has never been more than a breath here. As he folds his uniform pants, his wife rolls over and fumbles for the bedside lamp. When the light comes on, she winces, screws up her eyes, and rolls away again.

"What happened?" she asks over her shoulder. She heard the call and knew where it came from. It's unusual for him to be called out in the night except, these last two or three years, to the Wollastons'.

"George Wollaston's dead."

She turns over and holds a hand up to shade her eyes. "Dead? What do you mean 'dead'? How?"

"Dead as a haddock, Nancy. Lying stretched out like a starfish at the foot of them steps out back of his house. Same kind of fall as before, only this time he broke his neck. Webber and James are there. They'll wait for Wilcox. It's the end of an era."

Nancy props herself up on an elbow. In his wife's sleep-rumpled face, Eliot sees the girl she was in their high school class more than thirty years ago.

"Margaret there?" she asks.

"Margaret and Angie. Some old lady's staying with them."

"You think Margaret pushed him?"

He gives her a playful cuff. "Naw."

"Well...or Angie?"

"Now, Nancy..." he teases, shedding his shirt. "Though neither of them seemed exactly grief-stricken."

"Of course not. I'd have done it. I'd have pushed him." She pats the sheets. "Come on to bed. Turn out the light."

He adds his tie, uniform shirt, and skivvies to his folded pants on the chair. He switches off the lamp. In the sudden darkness, he sees the lingering square shape of the bed and the rectangle of the window beyond.

"I worry about James," he says.

She stirs again; he hears the sheet rustle. "You think James pushed him?"

"Now, Nancy..."

"I'd have pushed him," she says stubbornly. "I'm serious, I would. And I'd never blame either of those women or James or anyone else if they killed him."

Eliot has the last word: "All I can say is, if George had to get himself killed, I wish to God he'd done it in New York."

8

JAMES'S STORY

Webber noses the car up to the station house and turns off the ignition. James feels the older man's eyes on him. For what seems the hundredth time, Webber says, "I'm talking to you, Perham."

"Whatever happened out there tonight, I don't know any more about it than you do."

"That's not so," says Webber. "You know these people."

"*Knew* these people," James counters. "Past tense. Any *relationship* I had with the Wollastons ended ages ago." He opens the door and slides out of the car, leaving Webber to follow him up the narrow steps.

All eyes and a big smile, the new dispatcher says, "What happened?" The night, with its brilliant moon, has had its share of fights and domestics and car chases, but the Wollaston call was her big item.

"Dead as a smelt," Webber tells her. To James he says severely, "You're a cop. You *have to* talk about it."

James busies himself with putting up the radio and signing it in. Without meeting Webber's eyes, he hands over his book. The older man flicks through it. James hears the scratch of the pen signing his report.

"Listen, Perham," he says as he gives back the book. "You wouldn't be on midnights if Sprague wasn't sick. You and I were down there at 24:00 and he was all right then. You told me he was."

"And he was!" James shouts defensively. "Are you accusing me of something? Listen. Those people are strangers to me like they're strangers to you. Now just leave me alone!"

ဢ ဢ ဢ

Normally, when James gets home from work in the evening, his mother is asleep. When she leaves for work, he is asleep. But on this unusual morning he is too wound up to undress or even lie down. He flicks on the meager overhead fixture, but it soon looks pale against the growing daylight. He flicks it off and turns to the open window. The only thing he notices in the familiar scene is the dull glint of a pair of new metal trash cans in the neighbors' yard. They remind him of the Wollastons and how he came to know them.

ဢ ဢ ဢ

Angie Wollaston was the first summer person to be nice to James. How old was he then? Eleven? If so, she must have been twelve. She seemed much older.

"I'm afraid you can't play on this beach," she said.

He was surprised to see her there. He'd thought of that beach as his own even though he went there only once in a while. Before the summer people arrived, their properties were fair game for boys like James, as long as they watched out for the caretakers.

She said again, "You can't play on this beach."

He hardly took in the words; he was so captivated by her, an older girl from another world.

"See that?" she said, pointing to a trashcan. "Mom and Dad put that there to keep the beach clean. You never saw so much junk. We bought three last year, and they all disappeared, so now we have a rule: nobody can come here but us."

He thought her beautiful, in her white bathing suit, as she waved a tanned arm at the big silver-gray can. He wondered if he was on the wrong beach, if she was one of those summer people he'd heard about who live here year-round. On his way back to town, along the beach and through the woods, he puzzled it over.

He never knew why he went back. Even now he's amazed he had the courage. She was there the second time, wearing the same white bathing suit, sitting in a low chair and listening to a radio.

"You really can't come here," she said. "I'm sorry, but if we make one exception, we'd have to make exceptions for everybody."

The third time he went there, she ignored him, so he stayed. He hunted along the beach for bits of glass, like gumdrops, worn smooth by the surf. He'd lived in the town all his life and knew other beaches, but he'd never seen anything like hers. There was such a wide expanse of pale sand. Much of it had been imported by Angie's great-grandfather, James later learned. The sea was so broad and endless and so shimmering *bright* in the morning sun! It almost made him dizzy.

That third time, she asked him his name. He said, "James Perham," and she smiled.

"Well, James Perham, you certainly are one determined little boy."

"I'm not so little," said James, standing as tall as he could.

She sized him up, and a faint smile lit her face. "Maybe you're not," she said. "Maybe you're not."

After that he went there every chance he got, taking care to sit as close to her as he dared. He liked to watch her run into the water, swim about forty strokes, then run back out, slapping her arms around her shoulders. She spluttered, "It takes guts to do that in Maine, James Perham."

Once he ran in after her, swam further and stayed in longer than she. "I'm from Maine," he said triumphantly. "I'm used to these waters." His favorite thing was to sit on the sand, squinting against the glare, and watch her intently. He mashed black seaweed bladders between rocks so they popped like little firecrackers. She had him show her the trick.

One time a woman in a two-piece blue bathing suit came down the wooden steps from the house. She carried a basket and set it down next to where she then sat. She was Margaret Wollaston.

"Dad will be down in five minutes," she told Angie. "Who have we here?"

"This is my friend, James Perham," replied Angie. "I told him he could use the beach."

George Wollaston came down, wearing a faded old navy-blue shirt and rumpled khakis. James had never seen a man who stood so straight or seemed so sure of himself.

He looked at James. "Who've we got here?" he said.

Angie said, "This is James Perham."

George frowned. "Your old man wouldn't be Nate Perham, would he?"

James shook his head.

"Andy Perham? Ed Perham?"

Each time, James shook his head. George went to the basket and opened it.

"Here we are, James Perham," he said. "You know what's in this thermos? Martinis. Do you like martinis?"

"George!" Margaret scolded.

George said, "I know his old man or his uncle or somebody. Eliot Perham isn't kin to you, is he?"

"He's my uncle."

George gave Margaret a look as if to say, "See?"

"Your Uncle Eliot wouldn't have had a brother I never heard about, would he?"

James turned away. Until he started school, he hadn't known anything was wrong with having the same last name as his mother's family. George seemed not to care.

"Your Uncle Eliot and I are old friends," George said. "Here, James Perham, try this. It'll put hair on your chest."

James took a tiny sip of the martini and thought it was awful: it took his breath away and stung his mouth and throat, making him cough. But he liked George, who called him "Tiger." After that George said, "Well, Tiger, how are you today?" every time he saw him.

Angie told James she hated Maine with all its gloomy fog. She warned him not to bring any friends to the beach. "Dad'll never let you come back," she said. "He can be a real Tartar."

James said he wouldn't bring anyone; he didn't have many friends anyhow.

One day he found the beach empty. He could see, up over the bank, the roof of Angie's cottage and a few gable windows. After waiting a while, he climbed the steps. It was a *big* house with a big lawn up to and around it. He didn't see anyone, so he crossed the lawn to another set of steps that went up to a porch with a railing around it. He sat on the bottom step.

Angie came to the railing and looked down. "Well, James Perham, you really are the most persistent little boy I ever saw."

"I'm not so little," James said, getting to his feet. He stood as tall as he could.

She sized him up with that faint smile on her face. "Maybe you're not," she said. "Maybe you're not."

After that, he visited the Wollastons as much as he could every summer. He sat and looked out at the lawn, the stone benches, and the trees, pretending he was a summer person. He walked around to the driveway. Sometimes he found Margaret weeding flowerbeds at the edge of the woods. Sometimes she gave him a basket to carry. Then he pretended she was his real mother and that, after Labor Day, she'd take him to New York.

He was surprised to see an older boy on the beach one day, skipping stones while Angie was building a sand castle.

"Who's that?" James asked with a twinge of jealousy.

"That's just my brother, Tony. James, why don't you help me build this castle?"

When Margaret came down from the house to tell them it was lunchtime, Angie said, "I don't want lunch. I want to stay here and play with James Perham."

Tony walked in the soft sand, then ran up the steps after his mother. James noticed that Tony, on his way past them, walked in the same determined sort of way his father did. He had the same look of happy confidence.

§ § §

James hears the click of a light switch on the other side of the partition. An hour has gone by, and his mother is getting up to go to work. She opens the door and stands, staring at him. The room has lightened. It's five o'clock.

"What are you doing up?" she asks.

"George Wollaston's dead."

She shoots him a challenging look. Drawing her bathrobe strings close, she moves to the sink to pour water into the old aluminum percolator. She always eats something before she leaves for the motel. She'll have breakfast later with the others on the cleaning crew. She opens the refrigerator and takes out a pierced can of evaporated milk and a doughnut. She buys her food, and James buys his. Neither one touches the other's provisions.

He leaves the window and plants himself between her and the open refrigerator so she's forced to look at him. "I said George Wollaston's dead."

She reaches around him. "What do I care, after what he done to you?" she says. He steps out of the way, and she closes the refrigerator door.

ဢ ဢ ဢ

Margaret had taught James to knock when he went to their house; *she* knocks, she said, before she opens any closed door. One day, as he was about to knock, he heard George's voice. "I won't have a child of mine involved with a native."

Standing on that familiar porch, poised to knock on the door, James seemed to feel a falling away, as if the porch floor had become a slope he would have to climb. What he heard cut right through to remarks he'd heard all his life but hadn't wanted to believe: *the summer people will turn on you.* The kids at school said that. His mother had warned him. So had his uncle Eliot.

"That kid came to us like a stray pup, Margaret," said George, just inside the door. "We encouraged him. I'm as much to blame as anyone. But puppies grow up to be dogs.

All any of them want is to get something out of the summer people. They all pad their bills, and I'm sure he'll be no different. You've spent enough summers in French Haven, Margaret, to have more sense about this."

James yanked the door open: it was no time for knocking. They were in the hall at the foot of the stairs. They stared at him in surprise.

Margaret said a little too quickly, "Mr. Wollaston isn't himself today, James."

"What do you mean I'm not myself?" George blurted out. Then, as though seeing James afresh, he quieted down. A little too softly he said, "Mrs. Wollaston's right, Tiger. I'm not myself today. I'm sorry."

"You don't have to worry about me, Mr. Wollaston," James said. "I don't have any plans about Angie." Yet as he spoke, he recognized the lie. It was only when he heard himself say it that he admitted it to himself.

George smiled and held out his hand. "Shake, Tiger? Forget all this?"

"So long, Mr. Wollaston," said James, backing off. "So long, Mrs. Wollaston."

James doesn't remember going down to the beach, only that the tide, just going, had left the soft sand wet and sucking at his sneakers. He tripped on a pile of rotten seaweed. He can still feel its crusted surface give way. The rotted weed inside, slimy as old blood and warm from the sun, spurted up around his ankles.

"James!" It was Margaret. "James! Wait!" She'd followed him; he turned back. She ran down the steps and across the sand, and took both his hands in hers. She was out of breath. "Mr. Wollaston didn't mean what you think, James. He's not himself. Don't go, please don't go. Angie and Tony and I need you."

He loved her for saying that they needed him. Yet the memory returned — *summer people will turn on you* — to warn him it would be risky to go back.

"Please, James," Margaret said. "What you heard isn't the real Mr. Wollaston. This is hard for us all."

But he knew it wasn't the same for them as it was for him. He'd known there was a difference. That day he knew what it was for the first time in his life. He still has those old sneakers at the back of his closet, stained red-brown and crusted over with rotten weed.

9

SLEEPLESS NIGHT

As the tide floods into the inlet at the head of the cove, the surge runs up into the brook, then gurgles out again. Richard finds the sound as imperturbable, repetitious and soothing as Mrs. Moncure's monologues. Most nights he has only to lay his head on the pillow for it to lull him to sleep. Tonight, though, sleep won't come. He stares at the light trembling on the ceiling. It comes, reflected off the water, from the fish dock on the other side of the cove.

Lucasta said, "What's that there, outside the window?" With everyone drunk, it's amazing that anyone heard her. Toad would have because he doesn't drink as much as the others.

From the hall at the front end of Alderwood, one can see through glass doors onto two separate porches. There's a small entry porch outside the big front door on the driveway side of the house. On the sea side of the house, at the other end of the hall, is a broad expanse of porch out through a pair of French doors. One has a better view of the ends of this porch from the French doors of the living room and of the library, on either side of the hall.

Which window did Lucasta mean, or did she mean anything at all? Toad could have misheard her. At any rate, by now the slate of her memory has surely been wiped clean.

Flora said, "Won't hurt Dermott to wait, for once in his life." What was she having him wait for?

Thump, thump goes a boat, riding up on its mooring. On the ceiling the reflected light fractures and reassembles.

Many things seemed odd and now seem odder still when Richard thinks of them. It's such a set of coincidences: that George, after humiliating Angie in front of everyone, took it into his head to go out onto the porch; that Margaret happened to lock him out; that Flora was so strangely reluctant to go home; and...and...

Richard dreams he's carrying a suitcase. As he stumbles along, it grows heavier. At the bottom of his pocket, a key seems to be embedded in some gluey substance mixed with pocket lint. If he could extract the key, he could open the suitcase and, in the odd way of dreams, be rid of it. He wakes up, still feeling the burden of its weight, seeing in his mind the key in one of the French doors that give onto Alderwood's porch.

To cure insomnia think of a tunnel with some familiar, peaceful scene at the end of it — say a garden, a meadow, or a river. Richard pictures himself in Margaret's neglected garden... Sleep is out of the question. He throws off the covers, rolls over, and uses the momentum to get to his feet. He meets his own disheveled image in the window.

As in a double-exposed negative, he also sees a boat rolling gently on the long swell coming into the cove.

His house once belonged to a fisherman. All of it, including the working ell Richard added on, might fit onto George's seaside porch. It's in Horseshoe Cove, once an entirely local fishing community, now attracting the attention of the real estate market. He paid nine hundred dollars for what amounted to a fishing shack, using his first savings from his first job on the grounds crew at the French Haven Club. For twelve hundred more, after Crawford took him on, he added a strip of land to the south.

Crawford commended him, "That's the prudent Scot in you." Walking on the site, he scuffed the toes of his polished black shoes in the tarred, wiry grass among old Alby Kelly's heaped lobster traps. "You'll do well," Crawford prophesied. The core of Richard's house isn't much different from the days when Alby Kelly mended nets by the door. When the wind blows from the east, it still smells of marline twine. Richard insulated it and installed restaurant-size appliances in the ell.

In his orderly kitchen, he sets milk to warm, then takes a pen and a pad of yellow foolscap from a drawer. Across the top of the pad he writes, "Tues. Aug. 30, party at Wollastons'."

He has the habit, taught by Crawford, of finding a place to sit quietly while he focuses his thoughts on a rational solution to some problem such as a misplaced spoon or fork. Now he applies the same principle: what detail might he have missed the night he found George's body? He makes a note of everything he remembers, from his arrival at Alderwood to the moment he called the police. At last he tosses the pad onto the counter and massages his writing hand. His milk has boiled away, leaving brown scum in the pan. He was so engrossed that he didn't notice the sound or the stench of it.

He hears the surge in the inlet and a steady, familiar creaking begins at the far end of the cove. Alby Kelly's oldest boys are rowing out to their boat. Soon other fishermen will follow. Soon it will be daylight.

In his bed again, in the instant before he falls asleep, he sees George's face, dark against the white cushions of the big sofa on the porch. George seemed only a garden-variety drunk, not a man anyone would kill.

ဪ ဪ ဪ

"I heard the news," says Josephine, Richard's neighbor. She telephones as he is getting up. She reminds him of his mother, watching out for him. "Have you had breakfast? What if I come over and make it for you?"

By the time he enters the kitchen, Josephine has let herself in, and the house is filled with the fragrance of brewing coffee. Small and quick, she is the essence of efficiency. She's just taken up the pot and is threading a forefinger through the handles of two mugs. She is wearing her usual costume: a blue-denim skirt with frayed, bulging pockets and a blue shirt. She nudges the screen door with the toe of a sneaker. He follows her onto his pint-sized deck, and she kicks a chair forward for him.

"Writing your memoir, are you?"

He gives her an amused look. She knows everyone and everything within miles of French Haven. She knows Horseshoe Cove, Mountpeace, Wards Inlet, and Beardsley Hill. When she walks through his house, she never misses a dust ball. When she's home, she never turns off her radio scanner.

She places the pot on the broad deck railing. "Talk about it?" A gull, swimming close by on the dark water, cocks its head to turn a yellow eye on her and Richard.

In the clear morning sunlight, he looks out over the sparse, stubby grass above the seaweed-blackened high-water mark toward his neighbors' weathered sheds, bait barrels, and stacked traps and buoys. As he breathes in the familiar aromas of fish bait and diesel fuel and sips Josephine's fresh, strong coffee, his misgivings of the night strike him as exaggerated. Yet he is glad she's here. He has no idea how old she is, only that she retired from teaching school the year before.

"With that moon," she assures him, "I was awake half the night myself. Poor man. From what I hear, his family's better off without him. You have a lunch to fix somewhere?"

"Lucasta Forbush's."

Josephine acknowledges this news by compressing her lips sympathetically, as though she had a bite of a sour apple.

"You know what upsets me on top of everything else?" he says, "Flora acted funny."

"Flora has reason to act funny. What do you know about her?"

"Not much. She's the best waitress I have. She's married to a *rat*."

Within moments Josephine is stepping across the railing at the end of his deck and onto her own small porch. She comes back carrying a manila folder. "Have a look at these," she says. "I imagine George left her something in his will."

"George? Leave Flora something?"

She gives him the look a gossip gives the uninformed. "You don't know about George and Flora?"

Richard says he can't imagine it.

"I don't mean that. I should have said 'George and her first husband.'"

"Worse," says Richard.

"I don't mean that either." She hands him a class picture from the folder. "Here's her fifth-grade class. Flora's the one in the front row."

Richard follows her pointing finger. "That's *Flora*?"

"That's Flora. She was pretty. And here's Tim. He's the one I meant — her first husband."

Richard thinks, judging from the faded old class photograph, Flora's first husband was a decent, intelligent-looking boy, someone Richard would have liked. Flora was not only pretty; she looked like the mischievous sort of girl who would encourage dares.

"When you don't have lunch to fix, I'll tell you about it," Josephine says. "When you have time, I'll show you something in French Haven that'll surprise you." Her old eyes gleam.

Vacant mooring buoys and a string of lobster cars rise and fall tranquilly on the undulating swell. The fish dock lights still burn, weak in the sunlight.

"Flora was secretive," Josephine says. "The way she is now. You'll never get to know her. She was pretty then... fun...and popular."

§ § §

Richard's first intuition was no more than the uneasiness that kept him awake most of the night. A subliminal glimmering, it registered just near enough to the surface of his conscious mind to disturb what sleep he did get. For better or for worse, it compelled him to write his notes. Now, after Josephine's good coffee and breakfast, it transforms abruptly into something terrifyingly certain. He stands staring out at the harbor. How is he to proceed?

He dials the phone, listens to the ring. Will she have any idea what's on his mind? At last she picks up. "I don't understand," she says. "New York? This time of year, won't you lose a lot of income? How can you let down your old friends?"

"Flora will be there, Mrs. Wollaston, and I'll get someone to help. You'll be all right."

Silence. He imagines her concerned expression...or would she only wonder?

She breaks into his thoughts in a curt, business-like tone he doesn't recognize: "Thanks for letting me know," then she hangs up. He's reminded of the sort of disingenuous smile that flashes on and winks out just as quickly.

He grimaces. It has to be done; a few more calls. The club... He'll fix that chowder since he's already bought the clams and all. He's ordered the mussels for the Whittleseys' picnic, so he'll have to do that as well. On second thought he really should be there for George's funeral reception: he'll call Margaret back. He'll cancel his engagements with old Miss Dowson...Lucasta Forbush... who else? Pris Armbrister. Then...he checks the list of his upcoming jobs.

Perhaps the information he needs, to begin with, will be on microfilm or hard drive at the French Haven Public Library.

10

RICHARD'S STATEMENT

Charlie Byfield is the grandson of Charles Byfield who founded French Haven's only newspaper, the weekly *Chronicle*. He continues his grandfather's journalistic policies. There's no national news, nothing beyond the township French Haven, Maine, which includes the communities of French Haven, Horseshoe Cove, and Mountpeace. There is nothing libelous to French Haven citizens or summer residents, alive or dead, no bad news, and no controversy. The disappearance of a tourist in 1978, off one of the French Haven Boating Company's sightseeing vessels, didn't make the paper. The body of an unknown woman, discovered by a Mountpeace gardener under his employer's rhododendrons in 1984, didn't make it either. Readers interested in such gossip should consult the big Maine dailies available alongside *The Boston Globe*, *The New York Times*, the *International Herald Tribune,* and other scandal rags in Casey's Convenience Store.

The paper consists of eight pages. It always runs the same columns, of which there are three of a social nature: "French Haven Notes" by Loretta Sawyer; "News and Notes from Mountpeace" by Ella Nolan (Charlie's cousin); and Webster Stour's "Horseshoe Cove Jottings." These contain up-to-the-minute reports about year-round residents of French Haven and the surrounding hamlets, including their temporary indispositions, their recent travels, and the birthday parties for their children, including what was served and who made the decorations. There is a weekly tide table; a retired fisherman's summary entitled "The Week's Weather;" a column of bird sightings; one of garden notes; and a police blotter that gives details of traffic violations and, without naming names, arrests for petty thefts and misdemeanors. In winter, a box on the front page describes the condition of the area's roads. A social calendar lists dates, times, and venues of AA and Al-Anon meetings, Boy Scout meetings, choir practices, annual bake sales, and the Lions Club's lobster dinner in August. That is the *Chronicle*, and it appears on newsstands and in French Havenites' mailboxes on Wednesdays.

After Richard cancels his appointments, he drives into French Haven and parks behind the stately old *Chronicle* building. He goes into its small, plywood-paneled front office to pick up a copy of the issue for today, August thirty-first. It won't be out in the stores until this afternoon. He feels a sense of schoolboy excitement, of holiday and escape. He stares unseeing at the canvas map of the county, dated 1878, hanging on the wall. He considers whether it would have occurred to Chief Eliot or Lieutenant Webber to check the *Chronicle*. If so, at least one part of the case would be clearer to them.

Tucking the paper under his arm, he heads for the town library. This building too is a relic, going back even further than Charlie Byfield's press, to a time when French Haven consisted mostly of farmhouses, hayfields, pastures, and a few rickety piers. The library's furnishings were installed by a Boston lady in the 1880s. An historical room bears her family name. There are photos of old fishing sloops and coastal schooners, bygone citizens, early boarding houses, and the earliest ferry. When Richard first arrived in French Haven, the historical room enchanted him. He passes into the library proper and approaches the desk.

"Nancy, do you have *The New York Times* on microfilm or hard drive?" he asks.

A handsome blonde woman of something less than medium height, Nancy is Eliot Perham's wife. She regards him curiously. "We don't yet have much on hard drive, so what you're after is on microfilm. That's upstairs. Would you give me a minute?"

As he follows her up the narrow stairs, he wonders how it all will fit. New York is an eight- or nine-hour drive, two hours if he flies. When will he go? The mussel picnic is tomorrow, then George's reception the next day. He'll get an early start the following morning.

§ § §

Richard hands his notes to Chief Eliot in the station house. He sees a few sheets of paper, some formal-looking report, lying on the chief's desk.

Eliot says, "Go ahead, seeing it's you."

Richard feels a chill: it's the medical examiner's report.

He remembers the clean, silent kitchen after George's body was taken way. Margaret and Angie sat side by side at the bare wooden table while he scrambled eggs at the stove. Mrs. Moncure, silent for once, sat on the opposite side of the table, her small face looking pinched.

The words dance in front of his eyes. "Body white middle-aged male" stands out to him. "Pulse none, bullet wounds, stab wounds none."

"Go on, sit down," Eliot says. "Take your time."

The wriggling letters have settled down. Richard reads:

> 01:47 Aug. 31 Went to residence George Wollaston Route 5 east of French Haven, Maine. Found there body white middle-aged male known to me personally as George H. Wollaston at foot of porch steps east side of house. Body lying on back, arms & legs extended, fully clothed. Strong smell alcohol...

He skims through a lot of technical details.

> Cause of death subluxation of the first cervical vertebra result of fall while intoxicated... M.E. A. Wilcox.

"Broken neck," Eliot says. "Sit down. It was bound to happen sooner or later. He wasn't holding the booze anymore."

Richard glances at few loose-leaf pages lying on the desk.

Eliot waves a hand. "Go ahead."

Richard reads the meticulous, childlike hand:

> Wed. Aug. 31, drove Charley One with PO
> Jas. Perham to Wollaston cottage Old Cape
> Road as per instructions Chief E. Perham.
> Arrived 24:05. Waited while PO J. Perham
> checked cottage. 24:17 PO J. Perham
> returned to vehicle.

It didn't occur to Richard that the police had checked on Alderwood at midnight as usual, although now he remembers Angie telling him James would be there. It's probable that, as usual, in the kitchen he wouldn't have heard them anyway. A page follows in Webber's report of calls to a fight and a collision. Richard skips to the next page.

Sickened, he resumes:

> 24:46 received call to go to Wollaston cot-
> tage. PO J. Perham and self arrived scene
> 24:50 found body George Wollaston per-
> sonally known to PO J. Perham lying on
> grass about 3½' from bottom of porch
> steps. Strong smell alcohol, fully dressed

except one shoe found about 4' from body.
No pulse. No sign wounds. 12:55 EMS
attendant Edward Barber and EMS Ben-
jamin Ludlow arrived at scene. Following rule pursuant to unattended death,
notified state office Augusta ME. 13:55
M.E. A. Wilcox arrived scene. 14:00
Wilcox pronounced subject dead. Obtained
instructions from deceased's wife to use
Layton's Mortuary. Observations at scene:
One spruce stair tread, painted, 1½" thick,
cracked through from impact. One section
stair railing, spruce, painted 2 X 6, loosened. Body discovered by Richard Grassie.
P Lieut. Asa Webber.

Eliot says, "I used to park cars at the Wollastons', four,
five other kids and me. George brought his old man's bottles out and boozed it up with us. Those were the days,
with all them big yachts lying in the harbor. Lanterns in
all the trees, sixty people sat down to dinner, more coming
to dance after the grub-swapping. I never saw George's old
man without a glass in his hand.

"George and his brother Lyle and some of us used to
go aboard their big old schooner and sail around. Their old
man had special places built into the bilges to hide bottles.
George and Lyle knew the places. During Prohibition he
ran booze from Canada — came back with a full load of
the stuff. He tied lobster buoys to the cases and sank them

out there in the narrows. After he'd cleared customs, and when the Coast Guard wasn't around, he came back and hauled them up. He had an old Pierce Arrow with special places built to hide bottles just like the bootleggers. At the mention of any of this, George's mother had a look on her face that would break your heart.

"When Angie got into trouble with drugs and all, George kicked her out. James and my sister took her in. I told them, 'You ought to have slammed the door.' I said, 'You ought to have sent her to one of her own kind. Miss Hardy would have been glad to take her in New York.' By then the booze had gotten to George's brain. I tell my nephew James that nothing George said at the end was from the George he used to know."

ஞ ஞ ஞ

Fred Pemberton heard about George Wollaston on the scanner in his kitchen an hour ago. As he was opening Watkins Market, Junior came sprinting up the street to tell him all over again, and now he's getting it from his aunt Nettie.

Fred inherited Watkins Market from his father, who'd inherited the place from *his* father, the kind of carriage trade grocery not much seen anymore. Behind varnished mahogany counters are displays of the specialty items the summer people look for but can't find at the A & P or Shop 'n' Save. Fred stocks dried Montana morels, *confiture des fraises des bois*, and dozens of other exotics. He's never without Dundee marmalade. In the freezer he keeps Cornish hens and Carolina quail. He depends neither on his own kind, nor even the tourists, for his livelihood but rather on telephone orders placed by women like Nettie for the kitchens of the summer people for whom they work.

A silence on the wire tells him that, after a long emotional ramble, Nettie is coming to a conclusion. "Send us six lamb chops," she says. "No, make that ten. I'll take home four for Bide and me. Did you hear about the boy George hired? One of them hippies you see down by the dock, he threatened George. He told me, 'Nettie, that kid threatened me.'"

"One of Angie's friends is he?" Fred suggests. "You suppose Angie got him to do George in?"

"Fred, don't talk like that about that poor baby. She loved George. She worshipped the ground he walked on. You can put in some of them little new potatoes if you have 'em. Margaret liked the ones you sent last time. You know George had welts and cuts all over him, and the porch furniture was all knocked over. Oh Fred, I used to wash his hands and face for him when he was just a little thing. He was like a son to me."

"Junior, come in here. Aunt Nettie just called about George Wollaston. She was going on something awful — I thought she'd never hang up. I have to go down to the A & P for lamb chops. Call Willis at the Shop 'n' Save for me and see if they got in any more of them little new potatoes he had last week."

Fred's route to the A & P takes him past the post office. He goes in to visit Ev Hardesty, a stamp clerk. "You heard about George Wollaston, I expect," he says when Ev comes to the window.

Ev's not usually a talkative man, but the few times he does talk, he goes on and on. He comes out and leans against the narrow counter. "Well, now she's free, ain't she," he says, "and she'll have his money besides. I could never figure why she stayed with him except for the money. He was just a grown-up kid. He looked at things like a kid. I remember the time he parked behind Billy Whitcomb's car on Elm Street there, outside of Casey's. Billy was inside with the rest of us. It was a hot day and the door was open. We all heard George say, 'Let's goose it.' The next thing we all heard was the most god-awful crash. Billy's fender was stove in, and George drove off. The next day George called up Eliot Perham, mad as hell. He said, 'I want you to come down here and see what some son of a bitch did to the front end of my car.'

"Let me tell you a story. I was drivin' on the Shore Road one night when who should I come on to but Margaret. It was midnight. She was walkin' by herself on the side of the road. I stopped of course. 'Nice night,' I said. To tell you the truth, I was embarrassed. 'Oh Ev, I'm so glad you come by,' she says, as if 'tweren't nothin' to her to be out there in the dark dressed up for a party, and in she hopped. 'It *is* a nice night,' she said, not a peep about how she come to be there. Well, we got down to the cottage, and all the lights was on. George was outside, pacin' up and down in front of the door. 'I've been worried sick about you, Margaret,' says he. 'Where've you been?' 'Walkin' on the Shore Road where you put me out,' she says. 'Ev here was kind enough to pick me up.' 'I never put you out,' says George, and he says to me, 'my wife's a big joker, Ev.'

"Next day I run into Chauncey Falk down to Casey's, and what do you think he told me but *he*'d picked her up too. Same thing exactly, middle of the night. She was walkin' along a black-dark road, no house in sight for miles, wearin' earrings and a long skirt and all that. I guess George did that to her after some of their grub-swappin' parties. He'd be drunk but he wouldn't let her drive, and she naggin' him, so he'd put her out. Chauncey found her on the other side of Horseshoe Cove, two o'clock in the mornin'. She never turned a hair, just, 'It *is* a nice night, Chauncey, thank you so much.'

"You know, my niece was in the emergency room with a mashed finger the last time George fell. The nurse told her Margaret said, in front of her and the doctor who sewed him up, 'I'm just sorry you didn't break your *neck*.'"

Fred feels both overwhelmed and deflated. All he wanted was to tell what he knows about George. He likes Margaret: she pays her bills on time, and she never questions anything. He turns away.

"Wait, I can tell you worse," Ev said. "One night I saw George's car drivin' down Main Street wide open with no one at the wheel. I mean that's what it looked like till he raised his head. He'd been duckin' under the dashboard to scare Margaret. She was in the front seat stiff as a pike, same as you'd be if you was on a plane and the pilot come back and sat down with you. George liked to scare her. He did things like that on purpose. My cousin Dermott's wife Flora can tell you stories..."

Fred is on his way out the door.

ʄ ʄ ʄ

Lucasta, holding the telephone in one powerful hand, runs her other hand along the needle-worked headboard of her bed. She worked the pattern herself of pink needlepoint. Actually it's gros point because she is an impatient woman. There are bouquets of white peonies knotted in pale-blue ribbon, the tails of which are fluttering and pinked at the ends.

"*Ghastly*, Billy, simply *ghastly*," she says. "Enid called me. After the party, she left her purse over there. When she went back to get it, the police were just coming down the drive. For Angie, she thought, or her drug dealer friends. She'd already found the purse where she dropped it in the driveway, so she didn't hang around to find out. I can't say I've ever cared for Enid, any more than you do, but we have to feel sorry for her. She had a sneaker for George. Billy dear, I can't tell you how I feel being the bearer of such news, but it occurred to me you might not have heard, out there in Mountpeace. Poor Maggie! I'll go down there as soon as I get myself dressed, or do you think maybe I oughtn't? I do seem to have overslept; I'm afraid I overdid it in the garden yesterday. Here comes my breakfast... Mary has put one of my new Frau Karl Drushki roses on the tray."

ʄ ʄ ʄ

Miss Constance Hardy always breakfasts on a folding table of varnished maple in her small sitting room. On cool summer mornings, the sun shines in through the small-paned windows and warms her knees. Her rose-colored Saint Andrews tweed and matching cardigan are well grounded by her stout, laced brogans. She's been up and dressed since six. She has no patience for women who lounge about in wrappers in the morning.

"Thank you, Enid," she says into the telephone. "That's very kind of you, but I'll go down there myself. Williams will drive me. No, I'm quite sure. Thank you so much, my dear." Miss Hardy is one of the few people in French Haven who likes Enid, because she believes it her duty to like all family members. Enid takes her driving, comes by twice a week for tea, and never forgets her birthday. Even so, Miss Hardy finds her trying. Just now, delivering the terrible news of George's death, she exhibited a depth of emotion Miss Hardy found embarrassing.

She rings the bell. When her maid appears, she says, "Agnes, there's been an accident at Mr. George's. I'm going over there."

Agnes too has heard the news; she knows that not only was there an accident but Mr. George is dead. Until Miss Hardy herself chooses to tell her, however, she says nothing.

Miss Hardy lapses into silence for three or four minutes after she makes her announcement. This is a common thing with her. Agnes uses the time to straighten up the already tidy room. At last Miss Hardy says, "Well, that's that," which signals the end of something and time to move on. Agnes turns to go.

Miss Hardy doesn't say "tell Williams to bring the car around" or "bring me my hat and pocketbook." These things are understood. Agnes has been with Miss Hardy for thirty years in New York and here. She knows the old lady takes in more than her family gives her credit for. She is well aware of how things have been these last years between Mr. George and his wife. Agnes never fails to be surprised by how much Miss Hardy understands, while the family goes to great pains to spare her.

11

RICHARD DRINKING

On the heavily scored chopping block in Richard's kitchen, shelled clams give off their pungent sea smell, sharp on the air, overwhelming the odors of onion and scotch whiskey. A glass stands on the counter where Richard works, an open bottle within reach. Richard thinks, *My father and George Wollaston were drunks, and Crawford succumbed to it in the end. Dermott Hardesty seems to be a pretty hard case as well. Many children of drunks drink or go on drugs. That's evident enough in Angie and Tony.*

Richard never heard about the circumstances of Tony's death, but he suspects drugs or alcohol. He remembers the change in the expression on the boy's face. When he was little, it was as sunny and open as an infant's, as confident and optimistic. In his teens he looked doubtful and then angry. Overwhelmed at the end, Tony finally turned to the false refuge the son of a drunk often resorts to in desperation.

Richard turns to the clams — hen clams — and the chowder he's making. He bought them from Lyman Smith, a reliable source. There's so much trouble these days about where to get clams; so many off-limit beaches, polluted flats, irresponsible poachers. Lyman Smith gets his from people he trusts, and his mussels come from mussel ridges and uninhabited islands offshore.

Salt pork is trying and chopped onions are frying in Richard's big skillets. He is proud of his clean, reconditioned Garland stove with its blue trim.

Drinking is the hazard of his occupation. He has succeeded where many of his colleagues have failed because he's resisted the temptation of the daily handling of open bottles. "Richard doesn't drink," his clients say. "He won't drink up your best brandy." Yet here he is, drinking his own cooking whisky. Crawford warned Richard, "Your enemy," as he waved a hand at the display of open bottles on a table set up on old Miss Isobel Dowson's porch. That was the summer when the old man himself succumbed. Richard often remembers Crawford's most frequent admonition during the last years of his life. "Do as I say, not as I do," he said with an ironically rueful expression on his pallid face.

Get hold of yourself, Richard tells himself. He empties his glass back into the bottle, caps it, and thrusts it under the counter.

But if a man needs a drink, he does: there's Dermott Hardesty to consider! Dermott makes his money from stealing rhododendron and copper pipe off the summer places, jacking deer, and selling short lobsters...or did until his license got pulled. He must know everything that goes on as soon as it happens: soon after Richard turned in his notes this morning, Dermott bearded him as he came out of Lyman's.

"What're you doin' tellin' my business?" Dermott said as he shoved his reeking, unshaven red face into Richard's. The cords of his neck stood out boldly.

There's also Luke whatever his name is, the kid George hired. Luke, who looks like an angel in a Christmas illustration, confronted him on Main Street. "You asshole," he said. "Don't think I don't know you're the one told the cops I was there that night."

Richard has chopped the clams; he shoves them aside.

"I never said that," he told the boy, who gave him a disbelieving look.

"Somebody did," the boy said, "and it wasn't anybody I know." Luke's final words were "watch your back, motherfucker."

The odor of frying onions competes with that of the clams. It is nearly too much, even with every door and window open.

No drinking from now on. Newspapers are full of stories of men killed for the mistaken belief that they'd given evidence against others. History is full of stories of innocent men and women brought down by rumor and misconstrued or circumstantial evidence.

Richard feels overwhelmed by the fatigue of late summer in French Haven. He can't concentrate. Ordinarily he enjoys his work; now he finds it burdensome.

ᕡ ᕡ ᕡ

Richard loved his father's rich whiskey scent. The odor oozed out of his pores; it was on his breath; it lingered faintly in his old sweater and in a room where he had recently been.

Striding the length of the worn carpet, his father bellowed,

> *"Leeze me on drink! it gives more*
> *Than either school or college.*
> *It kindles wit, it wakens leer,*
> *It pangs us full o' knowledge.*
> *Be it whiskey gill or penny wheep,*
> *Or any stronger potion,*
> *It never fails, on drinkin' deep,*
> *To kittle up our notion."*

In Richard's memory, it was always winter. Icicles fell from the house's eaves.

> *"A vast unbottomed boundless pit*
> *Filled full o' flamin' brimstone,*
> *Whose ragin' flame and scorchin' heat*
> *Would melt the hardest whinstone!"*

ᔐ ᔐ ᔐ

Richard wonders: that night, might Angie have climbed the porch steps to have it out with her father? Might she have pled for his understanding, for him to listen to her?

He should have paid at least as much attention to her as he did to Toad or that ditz, Lucasta. Wearing her Indian print dress would have taunted George, especially with its silver threads glistening in the moonlight.

George would have laughed.

A sudden, irrational impulse could have ensued...

But the children of drunks don't kill...they endure. Some kill them*selves*.

§ § §

"I went for a drive after that scene with the old man, Richard. I mean...after I touched down with you there in the kitchen, I had to do something, you know? I really gave the old car a workout."

Now, Angie might do that, Richard thinks, *but why is she telling me this?* He remembers being unable to move the Porsche that night. The engine was cold. He doesn't tell her that no one drove her Porsche anywhere. Then, he dismissed the incident from his mind. Now he thinks of it again and tries to bring it into focus.

Her casual manner strikes him as strange for a girl who lost her father only the night before. Moreover she's come to him at an odd time and place. He's busy unloading the Subaru at the back door of the club for an annual luncheon she surely would have known about. She knew he'd be busy. She looks distraught, as well she might. He feels seedy and unfocused after all the excitement of last night.

"What're *you* doing back here, Angie?" he says.

"Slumming, ha ha."

"You came to see me," he teases.

"No joke, Mom sent me to get lobsters." She jerks a thumb in the direction of the town dock. "I came by here, I saw you. Voilà."

"Say, Angie, I'm sorry... I mean that was quite a shock, losing your father like that. You all right?"

"Yeah... I'll survive." She chews her thumbnail. "When the cops came last night, you know, Richard, were you, I mean, outside?"

He tells her he was. "Help me carry the stuff in?" he says lightly, not knowing how to take her in–distress–but–not–distressed demeanor. He adds seriously, "How's your mother?"

"She's all right." She stands a moment more. Behind her, the old Porsche purrs. She turns abruptly away, her thin shoulders hunched as though carrying a load. "Well, see you around," she says, then climbs into the little car and takes off with a roar and a spray of gravel.

12

INTRUDERS

Jim and Jerry were classmates at the University of Maine. Now, as reporters for the *Portland Herald* and the *Bangor Daily*, they're taking time to catch up, leaning against a roll of snow fencing at the end of the ball field. Neither has managed to get anything from the Wollaston family or any of their friends.

"It's not *all* bad," says Jim. "At least I've been getting some local color. Anything about this place is good for my producer. I got some stories would singe the hair off some of these stuck-up summer people.

A car is approaching; its tires hum on the pavement. It's a silver BMW with a newly painted front fender. At the wheel is a blonde bombshell of a society queen. She brings her car to a stop and fixes her prominent, pale eyes imperiously on the media men. She flairs out her nostrils as she draws in a breath to speak.

"You people stay out of my woods, or I'll have you arrested," she says. "I've called the police: they know who you are." She raises her chin and fixes them with a withering glare, then bombs off with a squeal of rubber.

"God, what a bitch," says Jim. "Talk about stuck-up!"

"You got *that* right."

"They sure aren't letting us anywhere near 'em..."

ၯ ၯ ၯ

Fog drifts in wisps between the sightseeing boat and the cottages across the pewter-colored water. Droplets glaze the faces of the passengers. Buzzy Smallwood bawls into the microphone, "The captain is doin' you a favor, folks. He's goin' in real close just for you, to show you where it happened. He's riskin' his license for you. You wouldn't want the owners to find out, would you?"

All this is part of Buzzy's act. Actually he owns a share of the company along with his five brothers, including the "captain." There's no risk for any sort of medium draft vessel going into the cove.

Buzzy, a husky man in his thirties, has the roundish, innocent-looking Smallwood face and a deep red-brown sunburn. He continues: "Now look at the big cottage just comin' into sight from behind them trees. That's where it happened. He fell off that long porch on the left side of the house. Look now, here it comes."

A woman at Buzzy's elbow has complained since they left the sunny town dock. She bursts out, "You say 'look, that's where it happened,' but how can we look when we can't see anything? You never said there'd be fog." The woman is wearing a sleeveless print dress that's limp from the damp air. Buzzy pegs her accent as Midwestern. "This is supposed to be *summer*," she says bitterly. "Nobody said it would be *cold*. I don't care *where* he fell or *what* happened: I'm *freezing!*"

Buzzy looks slyly at his other passengers. "Fog?" he says with a grin. "You call this *fog*?" The vessel idles near the shore. "Now, all of you keep an eye on the porch," Buzzy says. "Someone's there... That's Margaret Wollaston. A woman like her is used to fog."

It's true: someone has appeared on the porch. Between the drifting shreds of mist, Buzzy and his flock see the figure come to the railing and stand for a moment, looking toward them. Ashore, the sun is shining and shows that the slender figure is wearing a sweater. She turns and goes back into the house.

Buzzy draws the microphone dramatically close to his mouth and lowers his voice to a stage whisper. "That was her all right, but we'd better move on. I 'magine she don't like to hear herself talked about, specially not now. Some people say maybe she done it. What do you think? If you quote me, I'll deny it.

"All around in here" — he waves an arm around the cove — "is where, in the old days, the Robber Barons used to come to rest up from makin' all their money. Over on that side is where the Hardys kept their big steam yacht, *Andante*. Over there, that granite pier used to be the end of the dock where J.P. Morgan tied up his steam yacht, *Corsair*. He came to visit George Wollaston's grandpa Hardy about how to make money off folks like you and me. The library on Church Street has pictures of *Andante* and *Corsair* in the historical room."

The woman who complained, now with a blanket around her, still scowls. She mutters, "I don't care who did it. Anybody who owns a house like that deserves whatever he gets." As they leave the cove, the passengers gaze back at the shore for as long as there is anything to see.

Two men stand back in the stern, well apart from the other passengers.

Buzzy picks up the microphone again. "Here comes an osprey's nest, and up ahead we'll come to a cottage that will interest you. The man who built it tore down three castles in Europe and had 'em shipped over here. He was a Robber Baron. His great granddaughter uses it, summers. He had a steam yacht too, was a friend of old Mr. Hardy and J.P. Morgan, all o' them. That's in the historical room too. Now up ahead on the top of that dead tree is the osprey nest. See? It looks like an oversized bushel basket full of twigs. If we're lucky, you'll get to see an osprey or two." He puts down the microphone and walks aft toward the two men in the stern.

They wear sensible dark windbreakers and have bulky satchels slung on their shoulders. Throughout the tour they barely glanced at the sights Buzzy pointed out. Mostly they leaned on the stern rail and talked between themselves. Only now and then did they turn to look at the shore until they got to the Wollastons'. Then they got out their cameras, with big lenses on them, and listened attentively when Buzzy pointed out the cottage.

The boat idles along, nearing the osprey nest. Buzzy glances at his charges up forward. Except for the Midwestern woman, they look happy enough. After the osprey nest, the Whittleseys' stone cottage should keep them occupied.

"You guys from Maine?" Buzzy asks.

"We're from Maine," says one of them.

"In that case, this weather don't surprise you none." No response. "Stayin' long are ya?"

The men give him discouraging looks, and one of them turns to look out to sea.

Buzzy shrugs and goes forward again to pick up his microphone. "How many of you would like to see a seagull rookery? The park service won't let us stop there, but we'll slow down for you and those of you with good eyes or binoculars might see the nests and chicks."

"I'd like to see a seagull rookery," says a man with a guidebook.

"Me too!" says the boy with him.

"I got some good ones of her and the cottage," says Jerry in a low voice.

"So did I," says Jim.

§ § §

While Nettie and her granddaughter Crystal fend off calls in the house, Margaret, Angie, and Mrs. Moncure have retreated to the "old garden." At one time, not so long ago, it was a beautiful ornate garden. Its outline remains, of curving paths and stonewall borders. The reflecting pool, nearly entirely grown over, is ringed by a path of flagstones. There's a swelling of the path to accommodate a large old semicircular bench strategically placed to give an overview of the whole garden. Richard loves the place. Periodically, on his own time, he prunes back the overgrowth that wants to entangle the bench.

Richard has brought folding chairs from the house and arranged them to complete the circle started by the bench. In all the overgrowth, the spot is well hidden from the drive-way and the house. The three women sit facing inward like pioneer widows in a circle of Conestoga wagons in hostile territory. Margaret sits on a corner of the bench, Angie and Mrs. Moncure on chairs. Margaret and Angie wear pale summer cotton. The sunlight raises Mrs. Moncure's navy blue to a rich intensity. There are two empty chairs for Lyle and Enid Wollaston, who are expected.

Surprising things survive in the old garden. There's perennial heliotrope, sweet rocket, ginger, ajuga, sweet-briar, and Father Hugo's rose. Here and there an unexpect-edly persistent hybrid tea rose battles the roots and shade of the encroaching maples. This is the place Richard envi-sioned the night George died, when he hoped to trick him-self into sleep.

Margaret has been one of his most faithful clients for at least a decade. He used to catch a glimpse of her, weeding or cutting flowers in this garden, as he arrived for work.

His reverie is cut short as someone comes along the overgrown pathway. It's Enid, wearing a white skirt that shows off her bony knees. Margaret's sister-in-law picks her way forward with an air of distaste. As a Victorian lady finding herself in a jungle, she flinches at invading rose canes and ducks her head, with its girlish bandeau, under supple young tree limbs.

"*Here* you are," she says in her baby-girl voice.

Behind her comes Lyle. As he emerges among them, Margaret jumps to her feet. "Thank God you're here. Thank God."

He kisses her, then Angie, then turns to Mrs. Moncure. "And you're Mrs. Moncure," he says. The old lady sits placidly, her hands primly in her lap, gazing gravely up at him. "If I kiss Margaret and Angie, I ought to be able to kiss you," he says. She grudgingly disengages one hand. She bridles but allows him to kiss her on the cheek.

The brothers' resemblance is striking, Richard thinks as he always does when he sees Lyle. Not just physically but in voice and manner.

"Bad, and it's going to get worse," Lyle says. "Two guys with cameras jumped me at the airport. They want to intrude on us any way they can."

"When did you get in?"

"Just now. They looked pretty pleased with themselves, as if they have a scoop. And what's this about guards up at the end of the drive?"

"We have people on the beach and in the woods," says Margaret.

"Poor babies." George would have said that.

"Coke for you, Mr. Wollaston?"

"Richard! How are you? I didn't know you were here. Sure, I'll have a Coke."

The difference between the brothers is that Lyle has sobered up. George wouldn't even go on the wagon, however briefly.

13

CLAMSHELLS

Richard is setting up for a noonday picnic at Cynthia and Chris Whittlesey's. Cynthia is a stocky, sandy-haired woman in her forties. She served as ambassador to a Caribbean island during two Republican administrations. In Philadelphia, where they live, Chris paints society portraits and raises beagles. He spends his French Haven summers felling Cynthia's family's grand old trees for firewood. She inherited the cottage, a vast stone pile built by her great-grandfather. They tore down the ruins of three European castles for the stone to build it. After her father's death, her four sisters stripped it of any furniture and decorations they wanted. She never bothered to replace what was carried away.

Richard's impression of the Whittlesey household is that they take their meals at the club or picnic on take-out lobster rolls. Chris sometimes concocts a kind of slumgullion with cashews in it. "Clamshells in the Fireplace" is the local name for the house, though the old caretaker continues to have the sign bearing the original name, Eagle's Nest, renewed on the austere entrance gates. Kids usually steal each one soon after it's hung in place.

Richard sets up a serving table in the dappled shade of the big old birches. Cynthia, at loose ends until her guests arrive, joins him. "So tragic, all this," she says, "and so hard for you. I've thought a lot about that night. It does seem odd you never noticed anything."

He's made her a gin and tonic. She stands clutching the sweating glass in one freckled hand, frowning as she looks at the sea. "Everyone liked him so much" she says. "I had a terrific crush on him when I was fifteen."

Richard remembers that, from what he could tell, everyone did like George. With his Marine Corps officer's bearing, he was dashing, polite, courteous, and friendly. Only a few, aside from his immediate family, ever saw the darker side of him.

They hear a car door slam and the voices of guests arriving.

Cynthia says, "If anyone ever comes up with the answer to this, it's going to be you."

Richard conceals his anger. *This woman is clueless,* he concludes, clenching his teeth. *One minute she says it's a pity I don't remember more; the next she says I'll be the one to solve it. All right for her to say...* His presence at George's that night, and the notes he made and gave to the police, have had unpleasant consequences.

A breeze sets the trees' leaves trembling and lifts a corner of the cloth on Richard's serving table. He finds a clip to hold it down and hopes the distraction will prompt Cynthia to end the conversation.

ॐ ॐ ॐ

The party has worked its way down the hillside, its thirty-odd people nearing their morning's quota of alcohol. The Whittlesey children were given a midmorning lunch, but they're hungry again. At the last minute, Chris Whittlesey has a brainstorm: fill the children's little plastic rowboat with Richard's mussels *a la marinière*. Richard watches skeptically as the little craft — more of a tub than a boat — is dragged up from the beach and hosed out. It's as hygienic as most other setups at an outdoor meal, he supposes. He blocks it level on fallen branches, then pours the mussels into it from the big stock pot. He crouches down on the grass next to it to ladle them up. Flora, in her black uniform, dishes up grilled corn on the cob, salad, and buttered French bread.

A man wearing yellow cotton pants holds a paper bowl. "Very well to say there's always a first time," he says to someone, "but I can't see it."

Richard recognizes the yellow pants from past summers. The man is one of the Whittleseys' paying guests, a friend or a cousin who has sold or pulled down or rented out his own French Haven cottage. "I was in George's class at St. Tim's," the man goes on. "Lots of us were experimenting in those days. Everybody I knew was into hash at least, but not George. He said drugs would fry his brains.

He was as interested in Timothy Leary as the rest of us, but he got his kicks from booze."

"And fried his brains anyhow," someone adds. "Does anybody believe there's any truth in the story about Lucasta Forbush seeing somebody out the hall window? Oops, she isn't here, is she?"

The man in the yellow pants laughs and answers, "Not here."

Richard crouches next to the little boat to ladle up another portion of dripping mussels. This is the simplest of picnics with its scents of birch and trampled grass and salt air, the murmur of sated voices, and air of tranquil festivity. Yet Richard feels distaste for the work he ordinarily would enjoy. He feels impatient to be done with the job and oddly averse to simple tasks. It's now a chore to fill the trash cans with gnawed corncobs, used paper cups and plates, plastic forks and spoons, crumpled napkins, and mussel shells.

The remaining adults are examining their clothes for grass stains before moving on. The five children linger close to their little rowboat. Four little boys and a very small girl, they are being observed at a distance by their nursemaid. In exchange for helping fill the trashcans, the children propose that Richard helps empty their rowboat.

Richard scans their eager faces. The oldest boy, blond-haired Chris, eleven, is sturdy and responsible looking.

"We'll do it together," Richard tells the boy. When the last trash can has been filled, he sends Chris for his plastic containers. The leftovers will add to his supply of fish stock. The spot occupies a kind of plateau at the foot of a mild downward grade from the house. He positions the children along the down-slope side of the boat, each with a grip on the gunwale. He squats on the up-slope side, holding the containers ready.

"Slowly," he says, "steady..."

The small band, wearing serious, responsible expressions, tips up the little green hull.

One of the children shouts, "Look out!" There is something like a collective sigh from the children, and Richard feels a jolt and a splash of mussel juice cold on his shins. He turns around in time to see Dermott's old red truck, with nobody at the wheel, rolling quietly down toward him. It stops inches from where he crouches, the rusted bumper and fly-choked grille next to his ear. All but the little girl have maintained their positions.

Ten yards away stands Flora, wearing a white chef's apron over her black uniform. Holding the wire scraper she's been using to clean the barbecue grill, she's watching him with narrowed eyes. On the terrace above her, Dermott slouches negligently against the parapet, elbows propped on the coping stone, looking out to sea. Richard tries to decipher the expression on the big man's face, the same one he had in the Shop 'n' Save parking lot. It looks like defiance with, as much as he's come to know Dermott, surely amusement as well.

Dermott withdraws a toothpick from his mouth, flips it over the parapet, and looks at Flora. "Godfrey, Flora," he says, "you told me I ought to get them brakes looked at."

The boys goggle. The little girl is in tears.

"Want us to tip it up again?" says Chris.

"Sure," Richard answers. Over the sound of the containers splashing and gurgling full, he hears the voices of the Whittleseys' guests as they depart around the side of the house. None of them seems to have noticed the truck rolling down the lawn.

"That's somethin' for the books, now ain't it," he hears Dermott remark, directly behind him. Dermott is on his way, it seems, to retrieve the truck.

14

VISITING TIM

The morning after the Whittlesey picnic, Richard's determined little white-haired neighbor walks in and dictates, without prelude, in her brook-no-argument voice, "I'm taking you to visit someone; half an hour, no more. You can spare half an hour. This is in your own interest. The more you learn about George Wollaston, the better off you'll be. You've got yourself in the middle of something whether you intended to or not. You always say you're busy, but I'm not taking 'no.' Take the Subaru because I'll be staying there. By the way, you look awful." She turns and strides out his front door.

He knows he looks awful. He feels awful. The episode with Dermott has unnerved him. At least this morning she let him have his breakfast in peace. It's almost nine o'clock.

As Josephine walks back in, he has just put away his breakfast things and begun to pack utensils for his midday job. He hesitates: he's built his reputation on discretion; is Josephine a gossip? If he's learned anything during his working life, it is to keep away from gossips. In his childhood he saw enough of the effects of that on his mother. Yet he follows Josephine.

When he steps outside, she's already at the wheel of her old green Volkswagen. The moment he is in the Subaru and has the key in the ignition, she noses her way onto the faded blacktop from their communal grassy dooryard.

The road is little traveled. Overgrown on both edges, it curves past lonely stretches of rocky shore, which is skirted here and there by wild roses. They pass the occasional small house, barn, and mailbox. In a doorway a woman wearing an apron waves to them as they pass. They pass a car with Virginia plates, towing a camping trailer, and two RVs with folded beach chairs and bicycles lashed on the roofs. They turn onto a road headed away from the shore.

For a man who's lived for twelve years on the island, Richard barely knows some parts of it, including this road which he takes sometimes to vary his daily drive. Scrubby, second-growth larch and alder loop over the cracked roadway. They pass the occasional rusted house trailer. Ahead, at a higher elevation, appears a familiar red roof. It's some kind of nursing home, Richard gathers; he usually turns off before he reaches the place. At each curve in the road, the red roof grows more distinct. Two stories, glass and brick, the building has an awkward-looking addition on one end. Josephine enters a winding, hot-topped driveway and pulls into one of two parking lots. She eases the Bug into a space marked ELLIS, her family name, and waves him to a spot opposite.

The wind buffets the Subaru door as he opens it, and he smells the piercing resin scent of pine. Every bit of high ground on the island has a grand view, and this place is no exception. The eastern shore curves into the distance to the glittering rim of the sea. Sheltered from the wind, a dozen patients in wheelchairs sit on a sunny terrace. Josephine waves as she and Richard climb the front steps, but no one waves back.

"Incurables," she mutters as they reach the door. "Most of these people are." While she's talking, Richard reads the name of the place — Eastern Maine Long-Term Care Facility — over the doorway. The automatic double doors open for them.

The scent of flowers briefly masks the odors of medications and illness. They enter an elevator and rise to the second floor. The hallway is flooded with sunlight, or so it seems until Richard realizes the illusion comes from the effect of yellow walls and carpet in fluorescent light. He follows Josephine past a series of open doorways. She looks into two rooms and waves. Before a third she pauses and turns to Richard.

"He's blind and he can't talk, but he can hear as well as you can. He's been here for thirty-three years." She leads the way in.

The room is warmed by the same sunny colors as the hallway, lit up by a big window. There are two beds. In one lies a man evidently asleep. Beside the other a man in a wheelchair, wearing a bathrobe, appears to be watching TV. Two dressers are covered with a collection of objects, most notably teddy bears and greeting cards.

"Tim," says Josephine.

The gray-haired man in the wheelchair turns his heavily scarred and disfigured face toward the door.

"Tim, I've brought you a visitor," Josephine says. "Flora's told you about Richard."

The crippled man raises a palsied arm. His mouth opens and closes, but no sound comes out.

"I see Arthur has had his surgery," Josephine says with a gesture toward the other bed. "Richard can't stay, he has work to do, but I wanted you two to meet." Josephine sits down beside Tim. "His next job's at noon. He's the hardest-working man in French Haven. That big Norway maple by the Four Corners is starting to turn: it's going to be an early fall."

Tim scowls violently. In a kind of spasm, one crippled arm shoots out and sweeps across the table at his side.

"Your old neighbor on the hill is going to take up scalloping," Josephine says. "They say he's going partners with Duddy Connory."

Richard scans the objects on Tim's dresser: two teddy bears, a mechanical toy backhoe, a snow scene inside a glass paperweight, cards from Easter, cards from Christmas, birthday cards. The broad window shows the same view he saw from the parking lot.

Josephine says, "I have a story to tell you about Richard. It's pretty funny, but I can't tell it while he's here. I'm going to walk him down to the parking lot. I'll come right back."

In the elevator Richard raises an eyebrow at Josephine.

She gives him a reproving look. "I decided if you saw Tim you'd understand lots of things better than if I tried to tell you. Tim was Flora's first husband."

Surprised, Richard follows Josephine out of the elevator, across the lobby, and out into the parking lot.

"I thought Dermott..."

"You thought Dermott. That's another story. Tim was a twenty-two year old mail clerk when he married Flora. He's here because of George Wollaston.'

"George Wollaston?"

Richard remembers something partially overheard — a scandal involving George and an accident years ago. His aversion to gossip keeps him from remembering details. He and Josephine stand in the parking lot next to her VW. The sun beats down on the car's faded, scratched paint.

"Remember the class photo I showed you the morning after George died? Remember Flora in that picture? Come on, you remember. She was pretty, wasn't she? That surprised you, didn't it?"

Richard remembers, and yes, it was a surprise to think of Flora as that smiling, mischievous-looking girl.

"Remember the bright-looking boy who stood behind her? That was Tim."

Josephine opens the door of the VW, reaches into the back, and lifts out a bucket filled with goldenrod. She stoops, tilting the bucket to pour water out, then looks up at him.

"You know Pemberton's Hill?" she says. "How if you happen to be driving up the east side about a half hour before sunset, the sun can hit you in the eyes so you can't see a thing? Tim was riding his bicycle up the east side when George came driving up behind him. He'd been drinking, of course — he always drank, even then. Bea Bassett was with him, and I expect she'd been drinking too. George said neither one of them knew anything was there till Tim was on the hood."

"Good God!" says Richard.

Josephine is closely watching his face. She's wearing her usual faded blue denim. He sees her pink scalp through her white hair.

"Any scrape the summer people get into is news," she says. "Especially families like George's and Bea's. *The French Haven Chronicle* protected them, but one of the big dailies got hold of it, and overnight every paper and TV news show in the country ran the story. I remember the headlines. 'Wollaston Heir Involved in Car Accident.' 'Millionaires' Kids Injure Local Man.' The families were furious of course. On a personal level, I don't think George or Bea ever got over it. They were decent kids. Drinking was something everyone did in their crowd, what their parents did. Every summer for as long as I can remember, they've both come up here to visit Tim, and they've done everything you can think of to help Flora. Bea's a good sort, if you allow for the alcohol. Even if you don't, she does a lot of good."

Richard feels numb. The morning sun beats down on his head and shoulders. Behind him he hears some clatter. A couple of men are unloading what look like oxygen tanks from a van. He didn't hear the van arrive.

"Flora knew George would leave her money," Josephine says. "I'm sure Dermott knew it too and counted on getting it. Dermott is Tim's brother." She smiles grimly at

Richard's expression of surprise. "The day after the accident, Dermott tried to kill George. Took him by surprise, so he almost did kill him."

Far below, one of the big coastal schooners is bumbling along the shore. *Dermott*, Richard thinks; *he really was after me.* Josephine, with her connections around town, would have heard about both incidents; at the Shop 'n' Save and the Whittleseys' picnic.

For a man who sees Dermott almost daily, Richard knows surprisingly little about him aside from his belligerent, grudging attitude. The husband of Richard's most efficient waitress, he delivers her to jobs and picks her up afterward in his filthy old truck. What else does Richard know? Hearsay only, that he's a petty thief. Richard has seen evidence that he's a drinker. He may well be a man to hold a grudge for thirty-odd years.

"You're handicapped by not being *from* here," Josephine says. "If you were, you'd know Dermott has always eaten up every cent Flora has. And you'd know she bails him out of every trouble he gets into. When he gets picked up for stealing blueberry sods or digging up shrubbery off the summer places, she pays every fine. When he poaches clams or breaks into the cottages to steal copper piping, she always rescues him."

Josephine's figure, framed in the glare of sunlight on the blacktop, isn't too different from his mother's. Clara would have been Josephine's age if she'd survived. Clara, like Josephine, was small and energetic. Josephine is a retired schoolteacher. For a while after Andrew's death,

Clara taught school. Until her death, Clara did volunteer work, as does Josephine.

"I've got to go," Josephine says abruptly. "I come to see him every day I can. He looks forward to it. I collect news for him." She pats a shirt pocket. "I scribble things I know will interest him. I read to him. I bring him the kind of country stuff he remembers." She gestures at the goldenrod. "His family owned a little saltwater farm out on the Reach Road. When the water maples turn, I'll cut some branches and bring them in. I tell him what they look like. He almost never gets out of that room."

She touches Richard's wrist. "Now, about you. I've lived here all my life, I know a lot, and I'm safe as a church. If you want to talk things over, you know where I live."

Richard appreciates this. If Josephine were a gossip, she'd have given him some hint years ago about Flora's personal life. "What's this story you were going to tell about me?" he asks.

"The minute I said that, I knew I shouldn't have. It was about you and Dermott, the time you threw him out of Miss Isobel Dawson's for sneaking her sherry."

"I did?" Richard said. "I've forgotten."

"Maybe you have, but *he* hasn't."

15

GEORGE'S LAST PARTY

Of this big crowd of summer people in the sunny churchyard, only a few speak to Eliot. Most either don't recognize him or expect to see him here. His wife, Nancy, refused to come. "Why would I go to George Wollaston's funeral?" she said.

His jacket, taken from the back of his closet for the first time in at least ten years, is too tight. His cowlicks are slicked down, and his chin prickles with aftershave. He tells himself he's here for old times' sake, for the friend George had been to him, seemingly not so long ago.

The crowd funnels into the church. Eliot's nephew James, who arrived with him, has disappeared. Eliot finds himself beside a short, fat man who's saying, "Alice is coming back."

A tall, burly fellow, with a blue flower in his button-hole, says "I know she will. Alice loves you, don'tcha know."

Eliot knows the two men — William Abt and Welles Cordwainer, "Billy" and "Toad." They were at George's party. Eliot knows that Alice Abt will come back. A woman in her forties, she left Billy five years ago. She'll come back to him because she has little money of her own. He's heard, about her family, that "all those Stewarts lost everything they had in '29." Billy's name opens doors otherwise closed to her. She's assured of living comfortably as Mrs. William A. Abt of Philadelphia and French Haven, Maine.

Mrs. George Hardy Wollaston of New York and French Haven, Maine, Margaret may not have left because her family, too, lost most of its fortune during the Depression. Would she have left George, if not for money? Eliot has heard that she had considered it but, unlike Alice, she lacked the courage.

In front of Eliot, a fierce old lady in a printed silk suit scolds her companion: "You never *knew* him! George was a complex man. He had a rough childhood."

Moving with the flow, pressing toward the church's inner door, Eliot is swept past a group of young people bunched inside the vestibule. A resentful-looking blonde girl is intently studying a bronze tablet on the limestone wall. She's Angie's cousin Celia. They were inseparable as little girls, and it was hard to tell them apart. She runs a languid finger over the name "HARDY," George's mother's family, then "WOLLASTON."

Inside the church there's too much perfume, too many flowers. James is already seated near the rear. Cordwainer and Abt slip into place next to Lucasta Forbush and Bea Bassett — more of George's party crowd. They're a four-some, like gulls on a lobster boat.

The Wollaston family sits together in front: Margaret, Angie, Mrs. Moncure, George's brother Lyle, and his wife Enid. George's aunt, Miss Constance Hardy, and cousin, Pris Armbrister, are there with them. Eliot takes a seat next to James.

A man gets up from his seat near the front, walks up, and takes a stance facing the congregation. He introduces himself as a classmate of George. He tells an anecdote about sailing. "George and I were fourteen," he says, "and smoking our first cigars. We had on these hats we'd bought at Trimingham's, and George's hat blew off. He dived in after it, and the next thing I knew, I was by myself in the boat. Way off in the distance astern was this little speck wearing a hat, signaling what I had to do to pick him up. I didn't know the bow from the stern, but I picked him up. He was still chewing his cigar."

People laugh. The man goes on, "One time he and I skied at Tuckerman's Ravine. We started on our way back to New Haven but ran out of gas. We saw this driveway leading away on one side. 'I know where we are,' George said. 'That's my uncle Harry's place. We can sleep there.' 'It looks closed up to me,' I said. 'That's okay, Uncle Harry won't mind,' said George, so we pried off a shutter. In the middle of the night there was this awful banging. It was the caretaker with the police. The next day every wire service in the country had the story: 'WOLLASTON HEIR AND FRIEND BREAK INTO VERMONT SKI CHALET.' It wasn't even his uncle Harry's place. George laughed, of course — he and Uncle Harry laughed the whole thing off.

My old man didn't think it was so funny." Eliot can identify with the story, remembering the stone bench episode.

Other friends of George stand up and tell stories about school, youth, better times, kids' pranks, and drinking. One solemn-looking man, wearing a blazer with an emblem on the breast pocket, says, "George was the most generous man I ever knew." He talks about the tradition of philanthropy and volunteering in the Wollaston family and how George carried it on. When the last speaker sits down, a very old man with a pastor's collar totters up to the pulpit. He fumbles for his spectacles, rustles some papers, and begins, in a droning voice, to read the sermon.

Eliot hasn't the heart to follow the body to the cemetery. Abruptly he crouches forward and, as unobtrusively as he can, slips out of the church. Sunlight sparkles off parked cars all the way up and down the street. What could all those friends of George say that Eliot doesn't already know?

ဪ ဪ ဪ

Eliot parks the police cruiser under the deep overhang of trees in the back turnaround at Alderwood. Richard's Subaru is here with half a dozen other cars with Maine plates. They're probably Richard's helpers as well as those who are helping to park cars. Eliot plans to talk with Margaret, Angie, and Lyle, then make his exit.

He walks around to the side of the house that faces the water. He keeps going until he reaches the steep porch steps where George fell. The grass is still trampled where

Richard found the body. Unexpectedly the policeman in Eliot thinks, *What if someone pushed him?* He reconsiders: *Not likely. The poor guy only wanted to take a leak and get back into his house. He wanted to have another drink and go to bed. Margaret didn't know he was out there, so she locked up.* The gate, intended to block the steps from drunks like George, is now fastened. Eliot walks down to the beach. Pale yellow sand stretches away, glaring in the noontime sun. The sound of his heels on the wooden steps brings to mind a story he could have told at the church service.

He and George loaded the steps, constructed in one piece, into George's little open boat and sailed them, with hardly an inch or two of freeboard, to Hangman's Island out in the bay. There they sat till old Mr. Wollaston, having his noontime nip and gazing through the brass telescope mounted on the porch, happened to notice them.

Today there's not a boat on the water, not a gull on the beach. Behind Eliot, voices come from the open kitchen windows. That's Richard and his crew. He turns to look back. Off to the left, through the trees, is Lyle's house. That's another story he could have told.

Lyle's house was the old estate's gatehouse up at the head of the driveway. George and Lyle had it moved on rollers after their parents died. George and Eliot sneaked inside for the ride — dead against the law of course. After that, George and Lyle divided the property up. How old were they then? George must have been about fifteen and Lyle two years younger. They drew lots. The main house and half the land went to George. The other half of the land, plus six or seven outbuildings, went to Lyle. He eventually had an architect join and redesign the old carriage and gate houses into a nice, cozy residence. Eliot prefers Lyle's house to big old creaky Alderwood.

On the other side of the house, car doors slam. Eliot turns and walks slowly toward the sounds, keeping to the shade of the trees along the side of the lawn.

An old couple, being helped by their driver out of an aged Chrysler, pauses to stare around with eyes that express resentment at not having been invited to Alderwood for years. So Eliot surmises anyway. He's heard that, in the last few years, George and Margaret have neglected the older generation.

Eliot recognizes the Wollaston brothers' former sailing instructor who has arrived in a shabby Ford Taurus. Eliot follows him into the house.

Just inside the door, he comes close to colliding with Margaret. Wearing her dark church dress, she's coming from the library. Behind her comes Angie, wearing navy blue with white trim, and Flora Hardesty in her black waitress uniform. There's also a man in a dark suit, carrying a briefcase.

"Oh Eliot," Margaret says with a welcoming warmth. "Angie said you'd come. What would we do without old friends like you?" He appreciates her considerate nature. She looks pale and preoccupied: her regularly pleasant features are tense. Clearly, Angie's dress is a hand-me-down; its folds hang limply on her thin frame. The girl gives him a high sign. Flora keeps going, making a beeline for the kitchen. The man with the briefcase follows Margaret toward George's study.

Eliot hears more sounds of gravel crunching and car doors closing. The screen door bats and bats again. He watches curiously as each person comes in. One after the other, they speak to Margaret and glance uneasily toward the porch. Ordinarily there'd be a bar table set up out there, accessible from the hall. Now the double doors stand open, but the screen doors are closed. Blocking the doorway is a narrow table with a vase of lilies on it. Everyone looks relieved to stay inside.

Booze limbers them up. Little by little they raise their voices. Eliot hears laughter. The rich scents of bourbon whiskey and the food being passed around give him the eerie feeling that at any minute he'll see George. His old friend would have approved of the dress Margaret found for Angie. He'd have liked to see the crowded driveway. He'd have thanked Eliot for supplying the men to park cars, would have sent a bottle out to them. If George had been in charge of this party, he'd have had live music.

"Say, Eliot—"

He starts, until he sees that the familiar voice is not George but his brother Lyle. The two have always been so alike, with the same amused, the-world-is-my-oyster expression. Even now, on the occasion of his only brother's funeral, Lyle wears the same look. Their father had it too, and the same thirst George had.

Lyle nurses a glass of soda water. He really has sobered up if he doesn't drink on *this* occasion. It must be quite a jolt to begin his annual month of September in French Haven, the habit of a lifetime, with the funeral of his only brother.

"I saw you in church. Nancy here?" Lyle asks.

Eliot shakes his head.

"Remember me to her," Lyle says. A small woman seizes his arm and draws him away.

White-clothed bar tables are handy — something else George would have liked.

"I have found, Robin, that if one puts aside one's own emotional involvement and observes rituals such as these dispassionately, much can be learned. It is in the observance of ritual that we are given opportunity to know our fellow creatures."

Eliot recognizes the old lady he saw on the porch the night George died. She stands with an erect posture and wears a dark dress with a matching turban, as in an old movie. It's Richard she's talking to, but..."Robin?"

"On such occasions as these, one understands much," she goes on. "My father's funeral, for example, at Sweet Water, was not without its lessons. Sweet Water was the name of my childhood home, you know. On the day of my father's funeral, I understood many things for the first time. My sisters and I, unprepared as we all were for his passing, were astonished by its consequences. I learned a great deal about my family on that sad occasion. I fear my family learned a great deal about *me*."

In comes another aunt, from the other side of the Wollaston family, George's aunt. Miss Constance Hardy, a maiden lady wearing an old-fashioned long black dress and wielding a cane, stumps past the bar table. Old New York, with pearls the size of marbles, she wears large, sensible, expensive-looking shoes.

Mrs. Moncure, in her turban, frowns and takes a step backward. When Miss Hardy is safely past, she flirtatiously flicks out an ankle, closes the distance between herself and Richard, and begins the gesture Eliot remembers from the porch—stitching the air rhythmically at about the level of her ear.

He thinks, *I wouldn't miss this show for the world.*

"Nothing was the same among us after that sad occasion. Never," Mrs. Moncure says as if there'd been no interruption. She sees Eliot. "How do you do?" Her green eyes seem to be trying to place him. Richard moves on, and so does she, leaving Eliot without another word. She goes on in her soft, slightly heckling drawl, "I myself value family ties. I value morality in others. Strife within families is..."

"Eliot, you're smiling. What's funny? No, don't tell me." Lucasta Forbush flares her nostrils, and her large pale eyes give the turban a critical squint. "Would you say Mrs. Wollaston's aunt has fallen on hard times?"

"A different sort of time warp, missus," Eliot answers. He has yet to see Lucasta sober.

Elbowing past Lucasta comes the old minister. Apparently he christened George, and Margaret has coaxed him out of retirement. In a quavering voice he says, "I haven't been in this house since that other funeral...for the boy."

In the next room, Miss Hardy sits with her enormous feet planted foursquare against her chair's front legs. Her knees are apart, and a valley of black silk hangs between them to the floor. Near her a fist waggles an empty glass, signaling for a refill; Eliot recognizes Bea Bassett. Short, chunky, and terrifyingly outspoken, she's a disastrous drunk. Eliot likes her all the same. In the winter, when his police duties are less pressing, he takes care of her cottage. His cousin Freddy Lum, who works for her, calls him when he can't cope with her.

Something out of the ordinary seems to be going on in this part of the room. Enid Wollaston is talking, and people seem to be listening. It's unusual for people to pay attention to Enid. She looks to be in an odd mood and has a theatrical manner Eliot has never seen in her. Her little-girl voice has an affected, grating quality: "Why should I mince words?"

Eliot winces at the sound of her. Bea catches his eye and winks. George's next-door neighbor and closest confidante, Bea knows where all his bones are buried — even more than his contentious sister-in-law Enid. George confided that much to Eliot back when they were close. He wonders what Enid's going to dig up now.

She focuses on Miss Hardy. "Aunt Constance, I'm sorry you should have to hear this, but there are things that must be said. That night, I mean Tuesday, was a very peculiar evening. Ask anybody who was here. If you wonder why I bring up such a subject, it's because nobody else will. As we were all leaving George's party, Lucasta saw somebody out the hall window."

Miss Hardy's kindly full-moon face lights up. "Oh, go on! Lucasta! At the hall window!" An amused glint shines in her eyes, and her mouth hangs partly open as if in anticipation of a wonderfully funny story.

Lucasta frowns. "I did see something?" She looks puzzled. "What did I see?"

Bea brandishes her new drink at Enid's meager chest. "Before we get too excited," she says, "how about a few facts?" She takes another swallow, grimaces, and goes on. "Enid here claims Lucasta saw someone at a window. Has anyone here seen Lucasta at ten-thirty at night? She was smashed. I was smashed. We all were. We were tired. If I remember, Margaret kicked us out." Bea's eyes find Eliot's. "Has anyone here asked our chief of police where his boys found Lucasta that night? We're all friends here. Eliot, correct me if I'm wrong. Didn't two of your fellows find Mrs. Forbush seven miles down the old Cape Road at three in the morning? The BMW in a ditch and our heroine here passed out?"

Frowning, Mrs. Moncure makes her way around two elderly men who've separated her from Richard. "There is nothing sadder," she says. "Nothing."

"Gas gauge on empty, air conditioner blasting," Bea goes on, "steam pouring out from under the hood, radio playing 'Good Morning America.' All the way in first gear with the brake on, wrong direction of course. Snoring like a walrus. True, Eliot? Right, Lucasta?

"I don't remember that," Lucasta says defensively.

Clearly Bea is enjoying herself. So is Miss Hardy. She gawks at Bea, who beams back. "How about *that*, Miss Hardy?" she says. "Our Enid's going to have to do better than that, wouldn't you say? Shall we ask her what else worries her?"

Enid sets down her glass with a click. Raising her voice, she says tensely, "The porch gate was open."

"So?" says Bea. "George opened it."

Enid turns to the windows of the French doors that give onto the porch and says, "Look out there." Everyone looks. Down on the lawn, raking the grass, is the kid George hired. She points at Luke. "The day George died, he threatened George, who fired him right on the spot of course. Ask Nettie in the kitchen — she saw the whole thing. She saw George go out and tell the boy to put a shirt on. George came back in the house and said, 'Nettie, did you see that? That kid threatened me.' Some of you may not be aware that Margaret takes in some very peculiar people. She has since rehired him." She glares at Margaret. "I have taken the trouble to check on that boy," Enid goes on. "He has a record...in Philadelphia, not here. Don't forget, police in a place like French Haven..."

Bea thrusts her pug-dog face in front of Enid. "If you intend to turn this discussion into a character-assassination party against my friend Eliot here, you'll be sorry. For God's *sake*, Enid!" Bea is breathing in mild snorts, in the way of a pug, the way she does when she gets excited.

Down on the lawn, the boy pauses to lean on his rake and, shading his eyes, look at the sea. Before the party he was filling the fireplace wood boxes. Richard overheard Margaret say to Luke, "Just don't smoke pot here." Richard wonders if she hired him back after George's death because, like Angie, she has a soft spot for an underdog. Everyone on the island believes the kid killed George.

Two pink spots have appeared on Enid's hollow cheeks. In a thin voice she says, "My father knows the attorney general of the State of Maine."

"Attorney general," Miss Hardy echoes in a disappointed tone. Probably the words signal a change in the conversation to politics, in her mind. She swings her head, rather the way a bull would, toward Eliot. "Here," she says. Her big hands thrust her pocketbook into his. "Call Higgins for me."

Eliot is the chief of police, not a servant at the disposal of the party's guests, yet he understands her. She is one of the older generation who don't throw their weight around as the younger summer people are increasingly wont to do. He's happy to oblige Miss Hardy; yet in this crowd it stirs the old resentment. Eliot takes the pocketbook and starts off to find Higgins, her chauffeur. She is nearing eighty, and she's had a long morning — first at the church, then the cemetery, now this noisy party.

Margaret steps forward and takes the pocketbook from Eliot. Her face is dark with anger. Eliot is too upset to thank her. He nods instead and heads for the back of the house.

§ § §

In the kitchen, he's greeted by the aromas of crab-meat and chopped parsley. Nettie Pemberton, Margaret's cook and cleaning woman, grinds pepper. Nettie's grand-daughter stands gamely steadying the bowl with one hand, holding a fizzy dark drink in the other. From the back hall come sounds of ice cubes being crushed with a hammer. A door stands open to what used to be Margaret's kitchen garden. Eliot goes out and finds himself stepping carefully in a knee-high wilderness, overgrown with mint and chives. James follows. Sweat trickles into Eliot's eyes. He runs a hand through his hair and turns brusquely to face his nephew.

"You heard that? She's getting the attorney general down here."

"I heard it," says James.

Eliot bursts out in an undertone, "She's demanding an autopsy. Not only has she contacted the police in Philadelphia, where he comes from, but she's contacted the FBI as well. You know as well as I do the kid has a record. We have a sheet on him ourselves, and it's longer than her skinny arm."

James glances warningly back at Eliot. In the doorway stands Angie.

The girl, in her prim dress, steps out into the sunshine. "Don't mind me." Her eyes meet Eliot's. She breaks off a stalk of something and crushes it in her fingers. "Everyone knows Aunt Enid's a bitch." She giggles nervously. "Mom says she's a traitor to her class. Has anyone told you Dad left Flora a hundred and fifty thousand dollars?"

"Flora?" Eliot echoes.

The waitress stands in the doorway. It seems she too needs air. She fumbles in her apron pocket.

James turns to her with a crooked grin. "Looks like you're going to stay home now, Flora, and put your feet up."

She gives him a scandalized look. "Stay home," she fairly shouts, "with *Dermott?*"

16

A GOOD PLACE TO START

Layton's Funeral Home has delayed George's burial so a medical pathologist can go to work on him. The French Haven Hospital's lab is doing tests on samples of George's tissues. James sees no reason for any of this except, of course, that Enid has demanded it.

James and Webber have been called to a briefing with the state police homicide detective because they answered the call from the Wollastons' the night George died. James feels depressed.

Detective Le Bel is good looking in the way of many north woods loggers and trappers: solidly built, he has a rugged look about him, a bold jaw, and a swarthy complexion. This seems at odds with his well-combed black hair and immaculate, freshly pressed, uniform-like blue suit. His calm demeanor puts everyone at ease right away.

First off he says, with a hint of a grin, "I imagine all a local chief needs, in a resort town like French Haven, is to have a state homicide investigator land on him the week before Labor Day." He has a few questions, he says. What is Chief Eliot's view of Enid Wollaston? What is his view of the case?

"What we have here is a fart in a gale of wind," Eliot says. "And as for Enid Wollaston, if I saw someone dragging her down the street by her fingernails, I don't know that I wouldn't join in."

"Did the deceased use drugs?" the detective asks.

"He would never have used drugs," says Chief Eliot.

"There's always a first time," says Webber.

Le Bel considers this. "Was he a man to do himself in?"

"No," Chief Eliot says. "It wasn't the first time he fell off his porch, either. He was taken to the hospital a couple of times. He was a drunk."

"Open and shut then, eh?" says the detective with another hint of a grin. "For the record, how will the deceased's money be disposed of and what kind of money are we talking about?"

"You won't find out how much money he has," Chief Eliot says. "The State of Maine's full of resorts, and it's full of summer people, but French Haven isn't like the other places. The deceased and his friends are like the royals in England: they don't answer to anyone. They look at cops as servants to park their cars and check their cottages, and they don't think we're very good at either. To those people you'll be just a cop in a suit, detective."

"Cops in suits can pull some surprises," Le Bel says. Eliot is beginning to like this detective with his sly grin.

Le Bel is called to the telephone for a moment.

James becomes aware that something has been said, that everyone is looking at him.

"My nephew here might know about that," Chief Eliot is saying. "He's close with the girl."

"What's 'close'?" Le Bel says, looking at James.

"We're friends, sir."

"So you're close with the deceased's daughter?"

"She and I are friends, sir."

"And your friend's about to come into money."

The old fan, shifting direction, drones in a lower key. James is glad for the meager breeze it gives, for he's feeling distinctly warmer.

"I have looked at your report, Officer Perham," Le Bel says. "On the night of August thirtieth, you and the lieutenant here made a routine check of the deceased's house — something your chief has you do, I gather. If I read your reports for that night correctly, you did the checking, and Lieutenant Webber stayed in the car. Has it occurred to you that you could have been the last person to see the deceased alive?"

"I haven't thought about it, sir."

The detective raises his eyebrows. "You haven't?"

Chief Eliot intervenes. "I thought we agreed we don't have a case, Detective.

"Chief, that call just now was the pathologist. There were enough barbiturates in the deceased to kill a horse. Nembutal, most likely."

James becomes aware that he's stopped breathing.

"We've established that the deceased wouldn't have used drugs," says Le Bel. "What we have to think of is who slipped him something."

"Right," says Webber.

"Jeezum!" Chief Eliot exclaims under his breath.

"I'll take whatever you've got, Chief: photographs, notes, the file here, and I'll talk to everyone involved. I'll start right now with Officer Perham. Don't worry, Chief, your nephew's only one possibility. This morning when I walked in here, I noticed something about your nephew: he was upset. And I noticed that you, Chief, are worried about him. Now it may be something simple — he may owe you money, or maybe he didn't check in on his radio. But considering he's friends with the daughter who's coming into money, and he seems to have been the last to see the deceased alive, I think you, as a police officer, will agree with me that talking to him may be a good place to start.

"Officer Perham," Le Bel asks, "would you say you have a conflict of interest in this case?"

"No sir."

"If he has a conflict of interest, Detective, then so do I," says Chief Eliot.

Le Bel has hit on a tender point. Eliot does in fact worry, and quite a lot, about his nephew, if not for the reason the detective seems to assume. James never knew his father, who didn't stay long with his mother in the first place. The boy's mother, Eliot's sister, is indifferent to him. It's Eliot who has been there for him like a father. He has always been the one the boy came to when he was in trouble.

"Okay, Chief. But think before you answer this. I've been in this town one day, and I've already heard your nephew has a hot temper and he didn't get along with the deceased. I heard one of your fellow citizens say you're soft on the summer people. So I ask you again: in this particular case, would you say you and your nephew have a conflict of interest?"

Chief Eliot says, "Detective, my job's to cooperate with you, but that doesn't mean you can talk about one of my men any way you feel like."

Le Bel ignores Eliot, whose face turns an angry dark red. "Now, Lieutenant Webber, we know that while Officer Perham checked the deceased's house, you waited in the car. How long would you say he took to do the checking?"

Webber drags his book from his pocket, and thumbs through the pages until he finds the entry. "When Officer Perham left the radio car, it was five minutes past twenty-four hundred hours," he says. "When he came back it was seventeen minutes past twenty-four hundred hours. That makes, wait a sec...twelve minutes.

"That's a nice solid figure," Le Bel says.

Webber says, "I keep my watch set on military time."

"Good for you," Le Bel says and turns back to James. "Would you say twelve minutes is a fair amount of time for a man to walk around a house the size of the deceased's? Would that not be enough time, or would you say it's too much?"

Webber frowns. Eliot mutters sarcastically under his breath, "Now, *that* makes things some different."

§ § §

The central problem of James's life is that he doesn't know who he is. His mother tells him that often enough; so do his friends and Eliot as well. Facing the detective in the squad room, he senses right away that the older man picks up on it.

Le Bel smiles when, after saying "George," James corrects himself, "Mister Wollaston." James notices Le Bel's reaction when he hesitates between military time and civilian time. Sometimes he says "twelve o'clock" and sometimes "twenty-four hundred hours." It's not that he hasn't got it straight, but he feels nervous, being put on the spot like this.

James has heard that a good homicide detective will look for stuff like that. He wonders too if this one may not be above bullying. James has been bullied all his life about his close relationship with the Wollastons, particularly Angie. His classmates teased him, saying, "When're you moving into the *caw*-tage? Labor Day's coming — when're you going to New York with your friends?"

17

JAMES AND GEORGE

Before meeting the detective, James felt badly enough already, after his morning with Angie the day before.

She pushed her way into his apartment before eight in the morning. Her expression was the same as on the night, a couple of years ago, when she'd shown up wearing plastic holly in the zipper tab of her wet parka. She'd said in a pinched voice, a whisper almost, "James, can you and Tillie put me up?" This time she said in that same small voice, "Has Tillie gone to work?" He didn't answer; she knew his mother wouldn't be there. Angie was not embarrassed that she found him in his underwear; *he* was though. He wouldn't have been, he regretted, if things had been different between them.

"What's up?" he asked.

"Not here," she said. "Come for a walk."

Still zipping up, he followed her out of the apartment and down the narrow stairs to the alley. On the stoop he bent down to do up his laces.

"What's up?" he said.

She shook her head. She looked like she hadn't slept.

"You have some place in mind?"

"The point." She didn't wait for an answer but started off into the glare of the morning sun reflecting off the wet street. The point belongs to cousins of hers. There used to be a summer cottage on the site, but it was pulled down. Her cousins keep the entrance chained off but don't mind friends using the place.

James followed her past the ball park, out toward the entrances of the summer places. A few cars passed. At last they came to the great stone pillars that guard the entrance to the point. Angie jumped over the rusting chain and galloped down the weedy old driveway. Running along, she yanked the tops off whatever grew in her path, shredded the stalks and tossed them savagely away. She turned once and met his eyes with a glare that terrified him. She plunged on.

They skirted the old foundation and ran through overgrown fields among groups of grand old pine, larch, and spruce trees. The outer side of the point is open to the ocean; the cove on the inner side is a good fishing ground favored by kids and old men. James saw an outboard motor skiff with two old men, their hat brims over their faces. The men weren't aware of their presence. Angie headed for the granite ledge at the water's edge. They sat on a natural bench on the edge of the wide expanse of stone. He waited while she felt in her jeans pockets for something. An empty beer can hit the water with a tinny splash, and they heard the voices of the men in the skiff.

"She wouldn't be the first wife of a drunk to kill her husband."

"Prove she done it though."

The two voices were as distinct as if the men were there beside them on the rocks. James recognized the voice of Farnum Salsby, who'd worked for his uncle years ago.

"Oh gorry yes, all that money."

James jumped to his feet. "Hey!" he shouted. "The Wollastons aren't like that!" His voice echoed around the cove. Farnum and the other man shaded their eyes to look in James's direction.

"Sit down for God's sake," Angie whispered. "They can't see us."

It was true. Though the voices carried so distinctly, the men in the boat would have had a hard time seeing Angie and James among the huge slabs of granite in the glare of the sun.

Angie pulled a wad of paper out of her pocket and tossed it to him. He caught it in midair and flattened it out on the rock. It was a torn piece of newspaper, smeared and stained, with a picture of George and the headline "WOL-LASTON DEATH TO BE SUBJECT OF REVIEW."

"Read it," she said.

"'The August thirty-first death of George Hardy Wollaston in French Haven, Maine, is to be the subject of review by state authorities. Wollaston, fifty, a former Marine Corps colonel, was found dead on August thirty-first of an apparent fall from the porch of his summer home. He was a grandson of George Westleigh Hardy, an associate of Andrew Carnegie, and a descendant of Robert Wollaston, partner of J.P. Morgan. Initially local authorities ruled Wollaston's death accidental.'"

James handed the paper back. "That's your aunt Enid's doing," he said.

"That's only *The Bangor Daily News*," said Angie. "It's in *The New York Times*, it's on TV. Nettie knew about it before she came to work."

He was about to say, "Everyone knows it was an accident, everyone knows your aunt Enid's a bitch." But he saw she was crying. He scooted awkwardly across the rock and took her in his arms.

He thought she was too smart to be upset by some stupid by-the-book investigation. What was she scared of?

🌀 🌀 🌀

In the squad room, Le Bel's eyes are waiting when James looks up. He's been sitting in the same chair for what seems like hours.

He tries to focus on the present moment and the single point the detective is making, which is that he, James, might be considered a suspect in George's death. He should be thinking about the night itself, concentrating on the moments when he was out of the radio car while Webber waited for him.

George peered down at him in the moonlight, calling, "Tiger!" James's heart skidded to hear the affectionate old name, the familiar voice. Then he hardened himself: *I'm not Tiger anymore*. He looked at the high porch and imagined what could happen to a man in George's condition. He thought *I hope the bastard breaks his neck*.

The detective watches him like a cat watching a bird. Maybe the detective has the idea he'd carried Nembutal on him day after day, looking for his chance.

George's death hit James hard. He had believed in George, but George let him down. Still James looked up to George, respected him. He was still a father–like figure, in a way that only a lost boy could imagine. The rift between the two had not healed, and now George is dead.

As he walked back to the radio car that night, he wondered how such a man as George could have changed so completely.

Memories come back to him, milestones of the gradual change in George.

§ § §

Kerosene torches flickered on the Wollastons' beach during a long blue July twilight. Rolling edges of surf shone against the darker sand. George grilled steaks, working with the fork in one hand, a glass in the other, and the gin bottle wedged in the sand by his feet. He forked the steaks onto a board and carved them. Tony slid the charred slabs onto plates and added bread, scorching to the touch, from the coals at the edge of George's fire. Angie added servings from the big bowl of macaroni salad, and Nickie passed the plates around. Margaret sat on a blanket up against the seawall. She beckoned James to join her.

"We'll let the rest of them wait on us," she said.

George took an instant dislike to stocky, dark little Nickie. She worked in a bookstore in Cambridge, which was where Tony had met her. James sensed that Nickie was an outsider like himself. Her cheerful, blunt face glowed red-orange in the flickering torch-and-firelight as she threaded her way to the seawall to deliver their plates.

They were all sitting down and eating when George said, "Well, I had it to cut the steak. I put it right there on that rock."

"What did you put on the rock, Daddy?"

George ignored Angie's question and looked at Margaret. "You realize where that knife came from? Waddy gave it to me. Now somebody's taken it."

There was something strange in his tone, accusing and suspicious.

"It's there somewhere," Margaret said.

"It is not," George said. "It's not on the rock, and it's not in the sand. I put it down, and now it's gone. I want to know where it is. I want it back." He glared at her.

He's joking, thought James. Then it occurred to him that maybe he wasn't.

It was Nickie who found the knife; it had been kicked under a rock. The blade flashed in the firelight. "Here it is, Mr. Wollaston."

George brushed sand from the blade and ran a thumb along its edge. Margaret, sitting up on her blanket, warily watched his every motion. It seemed to James that she'd seen something like this before.

The next day they all were on the porch, lounging in the big, cushioned wicker chairs, facing the water.

Tony said, "Dad, last night you acted as if you thought one of us took your knife."

"I did what, Tone?"

"You acted like one of us took your knife."

"I did what? I don't get it. Why would I do a thing like that? Did something happen to my knife?" George pulled the knife from his pocket. Holding it by the lanyard, he looked around the group on the porch. His expression hardened when he came to Nickie. Margaret changed the subject.

ॐ ॐ ॐ

Last summer, George said, "I'm sending you to college, Tiger."

"College?" James was startled. No one in his family had gone beyond high school. But he respected George. "Okay," he said.

George ordered catalogues, talked up the courses, and helped him fill out applications. He took James to the admissions interview and insisted on a tour of the campus. "My friend Tiger here wants to know what kind of room you're going to give him," he told the dean.

A clean-cut, good-looking kid led them to a brick building and up to a room on the second floor.

"Faces south," George said happily as he looked around and out the window. But it was plain to see that the light flooding into the room was reflected from the dormitory opposite: the room actually faced north. James's incredulous gaze met that of the kid. James knew that George had to know north from south. All his life he'd been a sailor; in the Marine Corps, he'd been a navigator.

George failed to pay the tuition for his first semester. The oversight seemed odd; James doesn't remember why he didn't remind George the bill was overdue. It was probably because he wasn't all that keen on college. He was surprised, anyway. He got a job helping his uncle Eliot put storm shutters on the cottages he took care of, and Eliot promised him a job as a summer cop.

ॐ ॐ ॐ

James remembers the time when he overheard George saying he didn't want a child of his getting mixed up with a native. That didn't surprise him too much, though it hurt. It was clear by then that George had changed in some significant way. Later that fall George said, "Tiger, we don't see you anymore. What's up?" Not long thereafter, he said, "I don't understand you giving us the cold shoulder. It's not like you."

That was the year that news from Tony started worrying Margaret. She left French Haven, taking Angie with her. Afterward Angie told him about their trip. "We went to a place Mom knows where you can rent a cabin and be by yourself. She's upset...and I am too, James." After that it wasn't long before Tony died, and Angie was suddenly heavily into drugs.

As for George, he looked the same whenever James ran into him. He always looked as though he'd just stepped out of the shower; he even smelled of soap. His clothes always looked as if he'd just taken them out of the drawer. George's fastidiousness, a quality lacking in the other men James knew, never changed. There was no change in his appearance; but there surely was, behind the mask.

18

ELIOT COLLARS LUKE

What's this about barbiturates? Nembutal? Was it a laboratory mistake, a mix-up of samples? Nembutal in a man like George Wollaston? He drank himself blind, but he despised drugs. No. Never. Chief Eliot runs a hand through his hair, drags out a handkerchief and mops his face. What if the lab work is right? Eliot is familiar enough with barbiturates. They are common, easy to get, and used by lots of people.

Margaret, these last years, might understandably have used something to help her sleep. Angie is, or was, a walking drugstore; as a policeman Chief Eliot has had embarrassing moments with her. He imagines the medicine cabinets in a house like Alderwood where so many guests, so many servants, come and go. Through the years there have been so many parties. Lately, with Margaret not taking the trouble to keep the place up, such a house might contain anything at all in the way of drugs. Eliot remembers the kid George hired: *he* deals in pills.

Luke, that's the kid's name. Not only does he have a record in his hometown for dealing, but Chief Eliot's men have picked him up twice in the two months since his arrival in French Haven. "Yellow jackets" he calls Nembutal, "downers." Luke, the obvious answer. Poor George!

Enid Wollaston's story checked out, about Luke threatening George. Maybe Chief Eliot can get a confession from him. He jams his radio into his hip pocket, runs his fingers through his hair, and leaves the station house.

ᔕ ᔕ ᔕ

It's Labor Day weekend: tourists, wearing every imaginable getup, swarm thick as sand fleas. He crosses the street and makes his way to a boarded-up, abandoned building. It's a sad case that always reminds Eliot of another sad case, Buzzy Smallwood. On the deck of one of his family's sightseeing boats, wielding a microphone, Buzzy's like a bantam cock. On land, however, he seems to have an habitually defeated, almost servile demeanor. It's no wonder he's considered to be numb as a hake.

Eliot's mother, his aunts, and his grandmother bought thread and notions from the store that used to occupy the ground floor. He had his first tooth pulled by Doctor Bidwell at the top of the tilted wooden stairs. The building's current owner, Buzzy's father, Ledyard Smallwood, let the commercial leases expire and hired a contractor to pull it down. Chief Eliot had the pleasure of serving a restraining order in the name of a group of preservation-minded citizens. Out of spite, Ledyard and his sons retaliated by allowing kids to use the place as a flophouse. They probably hoped the kids would burn it down. Ragweed grows thick around and through the wooden doorsteps and all over the narrow dooryard. The building is a blight on the commercial heart of the town.

Chief Eliot enters by a side door, and waits until his eyes adjust to the darkness. As he feels his way up the stairs, he is greeted by the reek of candle wax, pot smoke, and stale pizza. Some light comes through the loosely boarded-over windows and shows him the shadowy outlines of sleeping bags. The kid he wants is not a yard from where he stands.

"Luke." He nudges the kid with his toe. No answer. "Time to get up, Luke." Another nudge, a groan, and the boy rolls over.

"Oh, it's you."

"It's me all right. Get your clothes on. You too," Chief Eliot adds as a second head pops up. "Anyone else, get a move on." He feels pleased with himself, taking care of two jobs in one. He'll clean out the place *and* bring in the kid. Now the trick will be to get a confession.

৯ ৯ ৯

Webber puts Luke in a chair facing the window. Afternoon light catches the boy full in the face. With golden curls cut short and skin smoother than a girl's, his squarish, baby face is the most angelic Eliot has ever seen. Eliot, leaning against the doorframe, reflects on how easily his old friend George would have hired such a boy. His khaki pants and knit shirt are immaculate, although rumpled from his having slept in them. Kids like him wash in the marble horse trough behind the ball field or in the kiddie pool behind the grade school, over the chain link fence. He seems to have the resources to keep himself well dressed. The report from Philadelphia lists his father's occupation as radiation oncologist in one of the city's teaching hospitals.

Chief Eliot interrogated the boy first, taking pleasure in the job. Then he allowed him to go, the idea being to let him feel confident, then haul him in a second time. Now it's Webber's turn. The big man gives off a deliberate air of cheerfulness and boredom. He makes a bulky silhouette, standing with his back against the light.

"The old boozer comes out where I'm working," Luke says for the second time in an equally deliberate, weary tone. "He goes, 'When you work for me, you wear a shirt.' And I go, 'It's eighty degrees, man.' Then he goes, 'Say *sir* when you talk to me, kid, say: eighty degrees, *sir*.' I go, 'Up yours, *sir*,' and he fires me. 'Where's my check?' I go, and he tells me to come back in the morning. I go, 'If you don't pay me right, you'll be sorry.' He goes, 'Is that a threat?' and I go, 'Look at it any way you want to, motherfucker.' 'You watch your tongue, you little bastard,' he says, and I go, 'I'll watch my tongue when I feel like it, shithead.'"

The boy's bored voice drones on. Eliot sees it all: the boy stays shirtless, then George, outraged, barges into the house and tells Nettie about the threat.

"He was mad enough not to pay me the next day or anytime," Luke concluded.

Webber winks at Eliot. "And that night you went back," he says. "You were stoned, he was drunk, and for the hell of it you slipped him something."

Luke cranes around at Chief Eliot. "Jesus, I don't believe this. You think I'd go back the same night for a lousy eighty bucks? If I went down there, which I *didn't*, and if I had something on me, I wouldn't *give* it to him."

"Okay, you didn't go back," says Webber equably. "Where were you?"

"I stayed in town and hung out. I went to the late movie."

"Name the movie."

When Chief Eliot asked, two hours earlier, "What movie?" the boy answered, "I forget," and Eliot ended the interrogation. This time Luke sits up, fishes in his pants pocket, and pulls out a flattened matchbook, a bottle of Visine, and a twenty-dollar bill. He lays these carefully across his knee and brings out a folded, dirty bit of paper.

"What's that supposed to be?" Webber says.

"The guy at the movie, the one who takes tickets. Call him, say it's Luke."

"Say it's Luke," Webber mimics.

Even if, in the remotest case, it turns out the kid did go to the movie, what proof would he have that he stayed through the show?

The voice on the phone is so loud that Chief Elliot quickly moves the receiver away from his ear. "Do I remem-

ber? I'll say! What performance? August thirtieth, last show.
How do I know? He told me. Just an hour ago, claims he
felt guilty. Yeah, claims he never meant not to pay. I took
the money, why not. No stub. He wrote his name for me,
yeah, his idea, right. Will I sign something? You bet I will!"

Webber gives the chief a triumphant look. Eliot thinks
it's as good as in the bag. The movie was a rerun of *Casa-
blanca*, nothing a kid like him would want to see.

"Beat it," Webber tells the boy, with another wink
at Eliot.

Eliot remembers Angie's version of the hiring. "Dad
put an ad in the paper, the kid showed up, Dad liked his
looks, brought him in the house, said, 'This is my wife,
this is my daughter, we keep the silver in here, over there's
the booze, my wife's jewelry is upstairs, first door on your
right, we never lock anything, you look like a nice kid.' No
references."

19

LE BEL AT ALDERWOOD

As Le Bel drives up to the front door of Alderwood, Margaret comes out to meet him. She cheerfully greets him when he gets out of the car. There's no sign of grief in this newly widowed lady. Suntanned and fit looking, she wears the kind of short, lightweight cotton skirt and sleeveless shirt the summer women here go for. On her tanned feet are colored kid loafers with contrasting trim, blue and yellow. She has intelligent-looking gray eyes and a good complexion too, considering the kind of life he understands they lead. Maybe she doesn't drink. The diamond on her finger is the size of his thumbnail.

"Would you like to go down to the beach?" she asks.

He considers it for a moment. "Why not?"

As they walk down the lawn, Margaret turns to him. "Did you know that Champlain landed here and established a settlement?" They walk along quietly for a moment. "That's what gave French Haven its name."

He turns to her. "Yes, I've heard something to that effect." He turns forward again. "I look forward to learning more in the town library...after we've solved this case."

"Of course," Margaret says as they approach the steps at the foot of the lawn.

Standing beside her on the beach, he again notices her diamond, as big as the button on his coat sleeve. A little breeze lifts the hair from her brow.

"May I ask you a favor, Mr. Le Bel?" she says. It dawns on him why she suggested the beach: no one's down here to overhear. "About my daughter."

What about her daughter? As if he could observe the workings of her mind, he sees it change: she has decided not to ask him whatever she intended.

Little white long-legged birds walk along the edge of the water, poking their long orange beaks forward and back with each step.

"It *is* pretty here, isn't it?" she says. "It takes a lot of managing. Every year the sand moves a little one way or the other. We deal with that. And the lawn gets eaten up..." With a wave of her arm, she directs his attention to a log wall built up against the bank. "We built this seawall to hold the lawn, but instead the sea works in behind it and eats away another few inches every winter. Now the state Department of Environmental Protection won't let us try anything more."

He says, "What about your daughter?"

She studies the pebbles at her feet, then stoops and selects a flat one. She straightens up and stands, weighing it in her palm. "This is hard for her, Mr. Le Bel. I'm sure you understand if you have children.

"I haven't...yet."

"She's been through a lot."

Whatever she brought him down here to say, he knows she hasn't said it. Maybe she's scared her daughter did it... and maybe the girl's scared her mom did.

She turns away and skips the pebble across the surface of the water. Five skips before it sinks; not bad, it seems to him.

As they walk back to the house, Le Bel's attention is drawn to the porch with its heavy festoon of vines. The steps bisect what seems to be a leafy green wall, solid below the deck and relatively sparse up to the handrail. The vine has climbed up the several columns and ranges along and onto the edge of the roof. As they walk past the end of the porch, Le Bel notes that the deck is at least six feet high.

They enter the house by way of the front door. "My husband's study," Margaret says as she shows him. At one end of a hallway off the entry, it's not a big room. A desk, a chair, and file cabinets occupy one end; a wing chair, a drop-leaf table, and bookshelves fill the other end. The walls are lined edge to edge with framed photos of school groups, ball teams, marines on parade, boats, houses, ships.

Margaret leads off to the other end of the hall. On one side is a wide stairway, landing in the entry. On the other side, the wall is hung with several memento prints of the

USS *Maine*. She continues out the open French doors onto the porch and holds the screen open for him.

On the porch, where the deceased was last seen alive, Le Bel observes three pair of French doors. They all have lightweight barrel bolts on the inside, and two are kept locked more or less permanently, according to the widow. The central doors, through which they've just come, are clearly the ones in regular use, so the two locked ones she speaks of are on either side. "We used to have them open all the time," she says with an odd look; almost, he would say, of wonder. She seems about to go on, but doesn't. He doesn't press her.

Le Bel notices fresh scratches in the painted wood sill under one of the "more or less" never-opened doors. He bends down for a closer look. Obviously *this* pair of doors has been used recently. Straightening up, he looks to see if she's noticed. If she has, he can't tell.

The porch's ceiling is tongue and groove, painted sky blue. He figures there has to be at least four feet of dead air between the ceiling and the peak of its roof. That would account for her not hearing anything that night, considering her bedroom window is just above the roof. That air pocket, plus the wind and her earphones, would have drowned out most sounds. Le Bel has heard about the wind from Chief Eliot. With so many trees so close to the house, the moving foliage would have made it hard to hear anyway. The caterer considered the earphones odd for a mother waiting up for a daughter.

"You always use earphones when you listen to music?"

Her clear gray eyes, startling against her tan, meet his. "Many times I didn't like to hear my husband come up to bed."

He respects her frankness.

Back inside, Le Bel turns around and looks out the door, surveying the porch. He considers that this is where most of the party took place — between the library on one side and the living room on the other. Houses like this were designed for parties. The large, high-ceilinged front rooms open into each other and onto the porch so that groups of people can circulate freely.

The library, properly named, is full of books and more books, a good many with the spines hanging off due to the sea air. The same moist air has swollen the supposedly never-used door so that, when opened, it scraped the sill. Besides the bookshelves, a bar and a stereo system are built into the wall. With sofas, chairs, and a TV as well as two great yacht half models, one on either side of the fireplace, it's a comfortable-looking room that has been used hard.

The living room is filled with sunlight, reflected off the water. Not the heart of the house evidently, although the fireplace has seen extensive use. It would be a good room for a party, as indeed the party in question started and ended in here. Through a huge doorway, spanning most of the width of the room, is the morning room. It looks like an extension of the living room except, instead of French doors and a picture window, there is a great bay window. Beyond the end of the porch with its overhanging vine-shrouded roof, it gathers more light than any of the other windows in these rooms. Le Bel imagines it must be nice to sit at the table here in the morning, especially in cool weather.

The kitchen is the first room they come to with anyone in it. A fat old woman named Nettie sits like a beanbag at a table, doing nothing. She's the one to whom the deceased reported the boy's threat. He'll talk to her.

Le Bel is taken aback at the sight of the Chinese room, with its dark-red wallpaper and varnished paintings of Chinese harbors. Margaret says, "My husband liked to have a reminder of his travels in the Orient." The plentiful light from the big picture window shows, in intricate detail, the objects with which the room is stuffed. There are lacquered Chinese screens, framed embroideries, varnished views of antique-looking Chinese waterfronts, and several wooden carvings of dragon-like creatures.

Margaret introduces Le Bel to Mrs. Moncure, "and my daughter, Angie."

The old aunt sits as prim as a schoolteacher in a '50s movie. "How do you do?" she says. The girl barely looks up from the card table where the two sit facing each other over a Scrabble board.

In this end of the room there are several shelves, piled up with familiar games: Parcheesi, Monopoly, Pictionary. The tattered boxes spill open at the corners. There are old packs of playing cards, racks of scarred and faded poker chips, dominoes, a backgammon table, and a miniature roulette wheel on another table. The room might just as well be called "the game room."

"Detective Le Bel would like to talk to you both later," Margaret says. She leads him off through the dining room. As he leaves the room, he feels their eyes following him. He hears a lawn mower somewhere outside and a vacuum cleaner somewhere in the house.

At the top of the stairs, the landing opens onto a broad hallway. The top half of the walls is of old-fashioned stippled plaster. Elegantly framed prints of English fox hunting scenes hang between doorways along the hall. Underneath is dark varnished wainscot, somewhat lower than waist-height. The stairway banister, across the hall, is the same height. To Le Bel it looks low for such a banister.

They go straight across the hall from the landing into Margaret's room. There is something in the caterer's notes about its furnishings. Le Bel ticks them off in his head: bed, desk, dressing table, chairs, chaise longue.

"I understand there was an open suitcase in your room that night," he says.

"I always keep a bag packed."

"You don't keep it packed now?" he says, giving her a challenging look.

She defiantly meets his eyes. "Things have changed," she replies, then opens a side door. "My husband's dressing room."

Le Bel is struck by the strong odors of bay rum and tobacco as she opens the door. This "dressing room" is nearly the size of a bedroom in his own house. It has an adjacent bathroom. She has an adjoined dressing room and bathroom as well. In the bedroom and dressing rooms there are several paintings in heavy old frames. Some of them are so heavily varnished, it's hard to make out what they depict.

He notices that she fiddles with the big diamond, moving it to the first knuckle then back again. He wonders if this may indicate she's hiding something, like a card player's tell.

Margaret moves on down the long broad hallway between closed doors. It's a string of bedrooms, obviously unused. The last door on the right is open, and they turn into the daughter's room. There's the usual stuff: twin beds, a dresser, a desk and chair. He smells the faint odor of... automobile grease. A red-plastic jerry can, a stack of distress flares, and a box of metric wrenches lie together on the floor in some sort of order. On the dresser is a collection of the kind of small boxes and vials drug users collect. These contain bolts and screws.

Margaret opens the door at the end of the hall to reveal another hallway, narrow and plain. This is the back end of the house, the old servants' quarters. She gives him her first smile, a look of ironic amusement.

"My aunt likes her privacy."

Le Bel smiles too at the idea of an old aunt living in the servants' wing of a big old house with lots of vacant front rooms. He counts nine servants' rooms and a large cedar linen closet. The tiny bathroom has the old fixtures including a claw-foot bathtub, wall-mounted sink, and pull-chain flush. The aunt's room is less than twice the size of the bathroom. It contains a narrow bed, a dresser, and a small table. Every surface is covered with china ornaments, perfume bottles, paperback books, and greeting cards.

Margaret says, "My son used to come back here." She runs her fingers along the top of a doorframe, takes down a key, opens the door, and stands aside for him to look in. The place is bare as a cell, with only a single narrow daybed, a standard cheap throw, and a chair.

"Your son liked his privacy too."

As she puts the key back, he grimly wonders about this family, whose old aunt prefers a cramped room in the isolated back wing of the big house; whose eighteen-year-old girl keeps wrenches and distress flares in her bedroom; and whose son retreated to the farthest end of the house, and later killed himself.

20

ANGIE AND MRS. MONCURE

When Le Bel returns to talk to the girl, the old lady has gone. That's fine with him. Angie sits where he last saw her, with her elbows propped on the card table, holding her face in her hands, staring glumly out the window. The Scrabble board remains unchanged.

"How'd you do with Mom?" she asks, turning to look at him.

She is pretty enough close up. She has her mother's eyes, but her narrow face is more like that of the old aunt. If she were his daughter, he'd buy her new sneakers and jeans and burn the old ones. He considers her a candidate to have killed her father. The motivations are there — money and anger — and opportunity. He's heard around town that she's a rich kid who likes to go with street people — who *did* like to go with street people.

"How did I do with your mom?" he says. "I got the grand tour. Houses like this are no longer private homes in my part of Maine." He pulls out a chair and sits down across the table from her. "We might as well start at the beginning, the night your father died. I understand you and your father had a disagreement before dinner, and you decided to drop out. After that no one saw you till the police arrived. Do you mind telling me where you were between ten o'clock and midnight?"

"I went for a drive."

"Do you mind saying where?"

"I drove out the old part of the Shore Road to the overlook, sat there awhile, then turned around and came home. I left the car out front to irritate Dad. Then I went for a walk in the woods. That's when I heard the police car."

"How long would you say all this took, the drive and the walk?"

"I don't know. I was upset. Two hours, anyway."

He gives her a skeptical look. "The police asked Richard to move your car, but he couldn't start it. It was cold. If you'd just driven it, it wouldn't have been cold, would it?"

At Richard's name her countenance hardens. "It wasn't cold," she says angrily. "Richard is a cook, and if he knew the first thing about vintage cars with chokes he would've had no problem."

With chokes, he thinks, *that's an interesting slip: if the engine were warm, there'd have been no need for the choke.* "Do you mind talking about your brother?"

She gives him a guarded look. "What do you want to know?"

He knows the story, or most of it. Tony Wollaston died two years ago in Boston. "Natural causes," the Boston coroner's report said. No one in French Haven believes that — unless suicide is a natural cause.

He sees how much the subject still hurts Angie. He feels for her. It's common knowledge that Tony's death came after bitter conflict with his father.

She gives him an ironic look and says in a stronger voice, "You ask, therefore you shall hear. Tony was Dad's shining boy. High honors, captain of varsity football, editor of the yearbook, perfect. Everything Dad wasn't. Everything Dad wished he'd been. Do you know Al-Anon? AA?"

He nods.

"Well, in our family Tony was the hero. You know, an alcoholic's family won't admit it has a problem as long as it has one kid who's doing well. Tony was that kid. Named for Dad of course, George Hardy Wollaston III — Tony so we wouldn't have two Georges; heaven forbid."

To Le Bel she looks defiant and worried all at once. She picks up the Scrabble scorecard and bends it back and forth.

"Everyone was crazy about Tony. Certainly Mom and I were, but I mean all our friends. I mean everyone who ever met him. If Dad was, he sure didn't show it. Whenever Tony asked permission to do anything, Dad's answer was always 'no,' but Tony learned that if he just went ahead and did it, he'd be praised. 'Atta boy, kiddo,' Dad said, same as when he was little. I hated it, but Tony didn't seem to mind.

"One Christmas he brought a bunch of friends home, and with them was a dumpy little girl from South Boston. She was bright, in his class at BU, pleasant enough, but not a Brahmin. Nickie was her name. She'd been here one night when Dad said, 'Tone, I want to talk to you.' So they had this talk. Tony told me about it later. He thought it was funny. Dad said, 'Uh, Tone, you know with women there are some you can get involved with and some you can't.' Right out of Jane Austen. Tony didn't have any serious thoughts about Nickie, but when Dad said that to him, he decided to go for her. He said it dawned on him that she was a nice girl and a friend of all of them in spite of where she came from; that Dad was way off base, judging her like that. He decided to show Dad.

"Well, surprise, surprise: he fell in love with her. Tony brought her here the next summer; then the next thing we knew, they were engaged. Dad hit the ceiling. I heard both sides of it. I heard Dad talking to Mom, and Tony talked to me. Dad said, 'If you really intend to get seriously involved with that girl, you've seen the last cent you'll get from me.'"

She pauses, quietly thoughtful.

"Then?" Le Bel prompts her.

"Then Tony married Nickie, and Dad cut him off. She and Tony lived in a furnished room in one of those old houses on the bottom end of Commonwealth Avenue in Boston. Dad had talked Tony into going in for architecture; but even though he had honors, architecture jobs are hard to find. By then he didn't want anything to do with Dad. He got a job in a restaurant behind Symphony Hall.

Nickie made money by drawing sketches of people on the sidewalks. She had a little money from her family." She pauses again. "Can you be happy marrying someone just to spite your dad?

"Nickie was a nice girl; she told Mom and me he got depressed. Nobody knows this in French Haven. I tell you because you'll find out anyhow. The Boston police found a note — maybe you already dug that up. Tony said all his life he'd tried to please his father till it dawned on him he'd never measure up. That's all. That was the note.

"Nickie was great. She came and stayed with us in New York. As long as she was in the house, Dad stayed away. He'd already started to change before Nickie. It's hard to tell when things like that begin. Ask someone at Al-Anon. Mom and I talk about that sometimes. You know, Detective, Dad wasn't always so awful. He was a wonderful father once...

"Dad blamed Tony's death on Nickie. When we got the news, he burst out, 'I never wanted that girl coming here!' He claimed her influence turned Tony into a hippie like his sister Angie. Mom and I know different. I know you talked to Mom. She blames Dad as much as I do."

Le Bel waits for her to go on. Obviously there is more she wants to tell. She gnaws on a fingernail.

"Those meetings, Al-Anon, you know. At first you think, *Who are these people?* You can't imagine how a bunch of strangers is going to help. Then you recognize parts of their stories and they recognize parts of yours. You find out some of them have been through worse than you have.

Mom and I talked Dad into coming with us one time. 'Haw haw, sure,' he said. He laughed through the whole thing. Mom was the enabler, and Dad was the dependent. Tony was the hero, and I was the lost child."

"Anyone on that list a murderer?" he asks.

She looks up, clearly shocked by the question.

"All that stuff went right over Dad's head too." On that note she stands up to go, but then asks, "Do you mind?"

With his hint of a grin, he sweeps his hand toward her and beyond, as though allowing her to pass before he does.

§ § §

After the girl leaves, the old lady appears in the doorway, right on cue. He has the feeling she's been waiting close by, possibly listening in. In her first sentence she promotes him to captain; shortly after she sits down, she changes his name.

"Sunderland. An English name, I believe," she says meditatively, as if they are old friends continuing a familiar conversation. She presses a finger into her cheek, as if to make a dimple, and regards him gravely with her green eyes. "Perhaps Welsh," she says, considering. "Possibly you know it?"

"I don't know it," Le Bel says.

Within moments he learns that Margaret Wollaston's aunt has invented other names. "Mellicent" is her niece; "Andrea" is her great-niece. "A version of Scotland's patron saint Andrew," she says, "one of the twelve apostles...in fact the first of all." "Geordie" is the recently deceased. "Robin" is the caterer, "Fiona" his waitress, and the young cop, "Justin."

He is momentarily taken aback by her somewhat bewildering presence. Her patient, gently hectoring drawl suggests she's a daughter of the old South. Wearing small pearls and some kind of fussy white ruffle at her throat, she sits as upright as a sentry and never takes her eyes off his face.

Between them, on the card table, lies the Scrabble game. It doesn't amount to much: two horizontal words, "SWEET" and "SAFELY," intersect one vertical word, "FRANTIC." He looks up to find the old lady's eyes fixed on his.

"*Frantic* is not a word I approve of," she says.

"Is that so?" Then that would have been the girl's contribution?

Either his presence winds her up, or it is her nature to talk. "One of the great novels begins, 'Every unhappy family is unhappy in its own fashion,'" she says. "I am a reader of the classics."

"Is that right?" he says.

"We can learn much from the great writers. I am fond of Tolstoy and the Brontës." As she speaks she makes small, circular motions in the air with one hand. "A knowledge of great literature gives one solace in times of trouble. My life, though, has not been without occasional reversals. Before literature, family is a great source of consolation.

My late husband, Mr. Moncure, was a man who enjoyed life's advantages, and so have I enjoyed them, to the full. The great tragedy of our age is the collapse of family, do you not agree?"

"Oh yes," says Le Bel. He remembers his own family, from a little town west of Lewiston, Maine. His parents, both dead now, spoke only French.

Moncure, he thinks; "*Mon curé,*" he offers in French.

"Mon-*cure,*" she corrects him, rhyming with *sure.* "My father was a country judge," she says. "In his career he had the opportunity to preside over some very interesting cases. He described the most interesting to my mother. My sisters and I listened of course. I have three sisters, you know. Ours is a fine old family, very old in our part of the world."

"And where would that be?"

"Kentucky," she says with what he takes to be a playful sort of pride.

He is quite taken with the way she says "Kentucky." Could she be flirting with him, in her way? She would have been pretty once. He put her age at seventy-plus. *Rich and plummy* strikes him as a good description of her drawl.

"Kentucky," he says, "Let's see, horses, blue grass, country music."

She looks offended. "Not all Kentuckians listen to country music, Captain. Now, we were speaking of my father. One case I recall was very similar to this. A man was believed to have suffered an accident, a fall not unlike my nephew's, down a stairway in his house. He was alone at the time: there were no witnesses. The poor man had misbehaved and had many enemies including members of his family, who were not all friendly with each other. His son-in-law requested the inquest. Do you see the parallel? Many individuals were interrogated, but no one was indicted, partly because the family was very prominent. Carr was their name — you may have heard of the case. Cameron Carr was the name of the dead man. As I have said, members of my family were old settlers. Our name, Warner, has been known in Kentucky from the earliest times. About the case I have described, my father was never taken in. Throughout the investigation and the comedy that attended it, he never believed for a moment there had been foul play."

"Too bad we haven't got your father here now," he says, poker-faced, as he thinks, *Every investigation needs its entertaining moments.* "I hear that the night your nephew-in-law died, you went upstairs with a tray and didn't come down again."

"Indeed," she says. "There was some unpleasantness before dinner. I felt my presence at the table would add nothing to the party. And then I had letters to write. I maintain a considerable correspondence with my sisters. You would like them — Stephanie, Tatiana and Penelope. Penelope is Mellicent's mother."

"Mellicent?" says Le Bel, momentarily bewildered.

"My niece, Geordie's widow," she reminds him. "I prefer the evening hours for writing, when the house is quiet. I have a small table in my room; I write by the window.

My late husband called me a night owl, and so I am. My late husband was a *rascal*. Mrs. Moncure begins again the odd motion with her fingers, reminding Le Bel of a pond where he used to fish, the insects that stitched the air above its surface.

21

RICHARD RECONNOITERS

As planned, Richard left early on the morning after George's reception. He had decided to drive, and so arrived in the city in the middle of the afternoon. He knew roughly where to go, and was amazed to find a place to park.

With everything Richard had heard about New York City, he imagined it would be glamorous. What he found was not at all so: he was bewildered by the constant noise and the feverish hustling of crowds of people. For one accustomed to the relatively easy-going life in eastern Maine, it was disorienting. He found himself looking up at the tall buildings, until it occurred to him that doing so showed him clearly to be a tourist. He was jarred by the thought that he would appear to be the same as so many tourists who wander around aimlessly in French Haven.

His search took him to a seedy-looking neighborhood whose buildings reminded him of the Smallwood building in French Haven. Asking for directions from the owner of a local diner got him into a friendly conversation, a welcome respite from the gruffness he encountered from people on the street. The man's name was Alexis.

"Do you know a Miss Witherspoon?" asked Richard.

"No, I but know a Miss Weinstock."

That figures. Richard suspected the name would be different from what Mrs. Moncure had told him. "That must be it: I was unsure of the name."

"I see her around all the time; everybody knows her. That's where she lives." Alexis gave a significant look toward a building diagonally across the street. It looked less shabby than the other buildings on the block.

Out on the street, Richard was again assaulted by the cacophony of traffic, shouting, and several radios playing at once. Crossing the street, he walked through a cloud of automobile exhaust. The soles of his feet ached from walking on concrete. He looked forward to getting the information he'd come for, so he could return to the clean air and bare turf of French Haven.

ဩ   ဩ   ဩ

"I lost a button and thought it might be here somewhere," Richard says as he shoulders his way past the sluggish bulk of Nettie, leaving her staring after him. The button is a lie. Richard always attends to loose buttons and sews them back when necessary.

As he passes the Chinese room, he sees Mrs. Moncure and Angie sitting together silently and rather glumly, it seems, at the Scrabble board. He pauses to observe them for a moment.

At the same time, Angie jumps up and her chair scrapes back. "I can't stand this, Aunt Beth!"

"Stand what, Andrea dear?" the old lady asks.

"Oh, Aunt Beth, all these questions, everything." Angie sees Richard and stops. Her incredulous expression seems to say, "Not you too!" She flees; he knows her well enough not to follow.

"You won't find no button in here," Nettie says, coming up behind him. "I just dusted."

"No kidding," Richard says. The thought of Margaret's fat old cleaning woman dusting anything seems unlikely, unless she's encouraged by the possibility of eavesdropping on the homicide investigation. For years now the real worker has been her granddaughter, Crystal.

"You won't find no button," she says again.

"Maybe on the porch," Richard says as he goes on.

No one is on the porch. Through the open French doors, he sees Nettie's broad, white-uniformed figure. She comes to the doorway and says, "You won't find it." After a moment, to his relief, she turns back toward the kitchen.

All the same, as if he expects to find the supposed button, he turns out the cushions of the big wicker sofa. He kneels and looks under all the wicker furniture. As though doing a kneeling push-up, he gets his eye as low as he can manage and peers along the floor.

To find Bea's missing earring, he should have come the day after George's death. He should have made a search that night. If he had not found George dead, he would have done it. The shock drove the idea from his mind. By now the porch has been swept clean. Richard asks himself how credible it is, after all, his idea that Luke may have taken the earring, George caught him, and a scuffle ensued.

The detective appears below him at the foot of the stairs. "Lose something?"

"I don't seem to find it."

The detective surveys him curiously. "Maybe we found it for you," he suggests.

"You found a button?"

"No button, I'm afraid."

§ § §

"Margaret, this is Eliot," the chief says into the phone. "We'd like to come down there tonight. We won't need to come in the house. You might hear us outside. You'll likely hear the car. We'll try to be quiet."

Richard, standing at Eliot's elbow, hears Margaret answer, sounding puzzled. "All right," she says. "Thanks for letting me know."

The lanterns, atop their stone piers at the head of Alderwood's driveway, shine feebly in the lingering twilight. Continuing down the driveway's dark tunnel of overhanging trees, they see the loom of the house's lights ahead. The scene brightens as they reach the openness of the lawn in front of the house.

"Left," says Richard, and they turn toward the "SERVICE" sign. Darkness descends again as they enter the thick maple woods at the back of the house. A soft glow comes from the window shade of Mrs. Moncure's Little Eyrie. Below it the kitchen and its adjoining rooms are in darkness. Margaret's room is on the other side of the house, facing the water. So is Angie's.

"Turn around, then park here," Richard says. They've reached the spot where he saw the truck the night George died.

Eliot drives around the little back circle before turning off the gravel to park on the turf at the edge of the woods. The two men get out and ease their way forward in the gloom. The leaves rustle in the wind. Richard feels its breath on one side of his face. It is the same wind that blew the night George died. The gray bulk of the house looms through gaps between the trees, and beyond is the paler gleam of the sea. The driveway lights of Outer Siberia thrust beams like fingers through the woods, casting the intervening tree trunks in silhouette.

Richard leads Eliot to the spot where he tied a white rag to a branch. "Stand here," he tells Eliot. "Give me a minute, then watch." He leaves Eliot beside the marked tree.

He slides into the Citation's passenger seat and fumbles a cigarette out of the pack he brought. He lights it and puffs until the end glows. He inadvertently inhales a bit and coughs violently, expelling the foul smoke.

Within moments Eliot joins him. "That's it!" he whispers. "That's it!"

Richard feels his excitement. Up on the road a car goes by, the sound of its singing tires muffled by the woods. Richard pulls out the ashtray and snubs out the cigarette.

He feels exhilarated. At the same time he feels uneasy in some obscure way. It's all too simple; he must have overlooked something.

"Well, I'll be damned," Eliot says. "It wasn't a reflection of the driveway lights. It was Flora, wasn't it, smoking as she waited for Dermott to come back and take her home."

Richard holds up a hand. "Tell me what you smell."

"Can't say I smell anything." Eliot sniffs the air. "Burnt match? Cigarette? Woods?"

"You don't smell the sea?" In the dark he doesn't see Eliot shake his head. "Wouldn't you think you'd smell sea, this close to the beach?"

"Not with the wind blowing southwest, toward the water. What are you driving at? It was the same wind that night."

"Right," says Richard. "The wind *was* southwest. But right here I smelled the sea. I noticed it the same time I saw Flora's cigarette."

"I don't get it."

"Neither did I... I mean I did and I didn't, in all the excitement. Think about it. The wind was from the southwest, but I smelled the sea...clam flats, really. It never occurred to me there'd be a truckload of clams twenty feet from where I stood. Dermott counted on George's crowd being too crocked to notice anything."

Eliot abruptly breaths out through his nose. "Jesus, Richard. Dermott was clamming!"

"That's it. The tide was out. I looked it up: dead low at five past eleven. I didn't smell Flora's cigarette. She smokes so much the smell was in my clothes, but I sure smelled low tide. Right here in the woods, with the wind southwest, I smelled mud flats. Dermott must've just loaded his haul..."

"And that's a closed beach." Eliot laughs. "I bet you there was some hepatitis going around next day.

"There was. Intestinal flu they called it, all around town."

"I bet you old Dermott busted a gut when he heard that siren. Of course he'll never admit it."

"And here's the other part," Richard says. "Angie was with him."

"How do you know she was?"

"Come on." Richard leads the way out of the woods. They go across the back turnaround and onto the lawn on the seaside. They skirt the house and its porch to arrive at the spot where he found George's body.

"Remember them two ambulance guys?" Richard says. "One of them said, 'The sea sure smells strong.' He said that after Angie came. I didn't think about it at the time. She'd been down on the beach with Dermott. When they heard the siren, he took off and she came to the house."

"I knew it, I knew it," Eliot says grimly.

"You guessed?" says Richard, disappointed.

"No. Oh no, I mean I *should*'ve known it. I remember now. Webber was filling me in when she came up. I smelled it myself. I never thought about it... Godfrey, Richard, Dermott! He was down there for two hours! And it's not as if he's a first offender. There's some big fine for that now."

After a pause, Eliot abruptly leans closer to Richard and lowers his voice, "What's to say Angie didn't kill George *and* help Dermott? She had the time."

"Because she didn't do it."

"You know that too?"

"I know that too. When Angie came up from the beach, she'd have brought sand with the mud on her sneakers. We smelled the mud, but there wasn't any sand on the porch. I remember thinking how slick the floor looked in the moonlight, and nothing crunched underfoot when I went out there."

22

LE BEL GOES VISITING

Flora is the Hardesty couple's sole means of support, so Le Bel visits her before eight in the morning. Dermott, in his undershirt in front of the TV, looks up and crosses his muscular arms over his chest. Flora, dressed for work in a black uniform, is pacing back and forth, smoking. She leads off with an attack.

"That lieutenant told me about how I said goodnight to Richard at ten-thirty. He said the police got there at twelve-thirty. He claimed Dermott's truck was there all that time and asked what were we up to."

Dermott's truck, he thinks. *That's a useful slip*. He's seen Webber's notes: they didn't say whose truck it was. Neither did Chief Eliot. The information they have from Richard is merely that he observed *a* truck parked in the woods. "What *were* you up to?" Le Bel asks.

"My husband and me, we don't take kindly to that kind of talk," Flora says. Le Bel notices some signal from the husband, which she ignores. "I know about them notes of yours," she bursts out. "I know where you got 'em, I know who wrote 'em up." She pauses to stub out her cigarette. "We were talkin', that's what. Does it say in them notes what kind of night it was? The kind o' night I never get to see cause I'm always workin' my butt off in some rich man's house. Moon-lit, warm: one night like that in a lifetime. And so Dermott says, 'Let's you and me take a walk.' Anythin' wrong with that?"

"Two hours?" Le Bel challenges.

Her pacing brings her to Dermott's chair. Ignoring his glare, she pivots on her heel and paces back. "Dermott and me, we didn't walk the whole two hours. We sat some. That big rock over by the end of the beach where the tide runs in — we sat there. And up in the field there's a stone wall. We sat there. My feet hurt, if you want to know." She thrusts out a foot, shod in a medium-heeled black oxford, for Le Bel to see.

There isn't any indication that she's in pain, nor does she limp as she paces back and forth.

The flickering light from the TV shows off Dermott's unshaven cheek. He twists himself around in his chair. "And what were *you* a-doin' that night, Mr. Le Bel?" he says. "Sittin' up studyin' how to put away some poor fella that never done you any harm, or home asleep in your bed? Or don't fellas like you notice moons like that? Maybe you don't get 'em in Augusta. Here all the tourists was out strollin' up and down, and parties was goin' on aboard all them yachts in the harbor, and tomcats was yowlin' their heads off in every backyard in town. I felt sorry for Flora not gettin' to see that. I said, 'You and me'll never get another night like this, Flora, so let's us take a walk in the field over there by Bassetts' and over by the old Hardesty homestead.'

"My family owned all this land down in here by Wollastons' and Bassetts' and all them big fields that's growed up in brush, and out past the end of the point and all acrost the road too, and all them islands that's owned by summer people now. When the British was blockadin' Boston, my family had full cellars here in French Haven.

"Flora said, 'Dermott, my feet are killin' me, I'd like to go with you, but I can't.' I said, 'We won't walk fast, we'll just take it easy.' That's what took us so long, you see. Well, Mr. Le Bel, that was *some* night. The wind was blowin', we could smell Wollastons' garden and Bassetts' garden and old Miss Dowson's roses, and we could see down inside the old cellar hole, choked up as it is. It was bright as day. I said, 'Look over there, them's the same raspberry bushes my folks planted, run wild, and over there's the apple tree my folks planted.' Flora here said, 'Dermott, this is worth the blisters I'm gonna have tomorrow. I'll never forget this as long as I live. This makes up for everythin'.'"

Dermott turns back to the TV. In the flickering light, Le Bel sees a grin on the curve of his cheek. Dermott swivels around again. "Now, Mr. Le Bel, if it popped into my head to give Flora a treat, and if she decided to let me do it, and if George Wollaston happened to fall off his porch around that same time, you can't blame us, now can you?"

Le Bel decides the time has come to pull the rug out from under him. "When the ambulance showed up, it seems you left in a hurry."

Dermott glances at Flora, then back at Le Bel. He hoists his bulk to his feet. "I know what it is," he says. "Eliot Perham told you I'm not his favorite customer, and that's the truth. So Flora and me, when we heard the siren, we said 'I bet you George has had hisself another fall or someone Angie used to go around with is over there raisin' Cain. If Eliot Perham finds us here, he'll get the wrong idea, won't he? Let's you and me scram.'"

Flora moves abruptly to the window and stands with her back to the room. Seeing her thin, black-clad form standing so rigidly, Le Bel thinks, *Her husband's version of the story has put her off...or maybe they've had a fight.* He wonders what it was about.

It seems to Le Bel that Dermott is a good candidate. He's not the type to use pills — but he imagines that a drinker would know how to kill another drinker. If the sister-in-law hadn't gotten into the act, he'd have got away with it. He may yet.

§ § §

Chief Eliot told Le Bel, "Richard is just a poor guy from the Maritimes who landed here without a cent. He makes eighty percent of his income in two months, July Fourth to Labor Day. Of course he's not alone in that. Some of the summer people hang around after Labor Day. A lot of them come back and open up their cottages for Christmas and bring guests. He also has what he calls his 'year-round summer people.'"

Le Bel wonders about Richard: his father was a drunk — died of it one way or another — so he's scared to death of alcohol, believes it's genetic. That makes two of them: him and Angie Wollaston. She's scared of the same thing. Richard was on his feet for twelve hours, serving meals at two different houses. Then he found a dead body as he was about to leave house number two, called the police, and was detained on the scene for at least another couple of hours. He got home at three in the morning with another big day coming up...and stayed up *writing notes?*

Could it be that he's protecting someone? The widow or the girl? It's more likely the girl: Le Bel has seen his face when her name is mentioned. If he's not protecting her, at least he's worried about her.

All right, says Le Bel to himself, assessing the situation. *Who would have wanted to kill the deceased?* The wife, the daughter, young Perham, Flora and/or Dermot, the caterer...but that seems unlikely. The hired kid's a likely customer; he's like an old-time con who knows his way around the jailhouse... His father may be able to pull strings for him, too.

It's that sort of influence, after all, that got the state police involved in the first place.

§ § §

Lyle Wollaston, some kind of advisor to the Commerce Department in Washington, appears on his porch, looking out of sorts. He's wearing a knitted shirt, khaki pants with a white cotton hat rolled up and stuffed in a pocket, and loafers with no socks. He starts off by saying, "My brother's death is probably a good thing, unfortunately, Inspector. My sister-in-law and my niece have been through hell these last years. I'm a recovering alcoholic myself. I know what my brother's family has gone through."

"Can you think," Le Bel asks, "of a reason why someone would want to murder your brother?"

Lyle glances at his wife, then answers, "I can see why any number of people might have wanted to kill George. I came damn near it myself. I don't know anyone who'd actually *do* it."

Enid Wollaston makes a point of keeping her distance while Le Bel talks with her husband. However, her whole skinny person signals, *Wait till you get around to me, Detective: you'll get an earful.* Looking at her, Le Bel remembers another investigation he worked on in which a couple with connections went over the head of a small-town police chief. There turned out to be a personal motive in that case. He senses a personal motive in Enid. Some old grudge on the part of this bony, coy woman with her baby-girl voice. While her husband talks, she makes a point of sitting in an odd, repressed posture in her caned chair. She holds her thin arms rigidly in a narrow V so her elbows nearly touch, wrists crossed, with fingers intertwined in her lap.

When Le Bel addresses her, she says only, "My brother-in-law was unhappy, Detective. People who knew him well understood the strain he was under; they loved and respected him. He confided in me."

"What strain was he under?" Le Bel asks.

She purses her lips and looks away.

"My wife is a nervous woman," Lyle says.

And she was in love with your brother, observes Le Bel. She is the one Chief Eliot refers to as "the clam." She made a big fuss as though she had something to say; now here she is being coy to the detective whose very presence is a result of her fuss. There's something corny and somehow obvious about this woman who demanded a state homicide investigation and has now clammed up.

🐚 🐚 🐚

Le Bel calls on Bea Bassett in the early afternoon. The little bulldog woman, with a glass in one hand, holds her front door open for him.

She waves him in and asks, "You don't mind if I finish my orange juice?" She wags the glass, tall as a milkshake glass and nearly full, spilling a dollop over the brim. "Offer you some?"

"No thanks," he says.

"Sit outside?" she says and leads the way through a long picture-hung hallway opening onto a terrace commanding the same broad view as that of the deceased. The two houses, hidden from each other, look out on the same deep cove. Le Bel, walking behind her, detects the sweetish fragrance of metabolized alcohol that oozes out of the pores of the hardcore drinker.

On the terrace a big fellow with pop eyes rises to his feet. Bea waves Le Bel to a painted metal chair and sits down herself. A maid in a yellow uniform appears with an embroidered canvas bag, which she sets beside Bea.

"Am I interrupting something?" the big man says. "Ah...I believe we haven't met, don'tcha know."

"Two birds with one stone," says Bea. "Stick around, Toad baby."

Welles Cordwainer. He was another guest at the deceased's house the night he died. None of the Wollastons' dinner guests have occupations in any sense Le Bel understands. "Fiduciary responsibilities, don'tcha know," says this Toad fellow. The tubby little fellow from Mountpeace who left the party early says he's "a trustee." The big blonde woman who ran her BMW off the road, this chunky little woman with the bulldog face, and her tall, soft-voiced friend are all divorced. Le Bel supposes they live off their divorce settlements; they probably have money from their families as well.

Bea parks her glass on a table, leans over the canvas bag, and pulls out a loosely knotted hank of orange wool. She unties it and begins to separate the strands. "So, detective, what'll you have?" she says. "Teenager axes parent? Wife strangles hubby? Handyman stabs boss? Waitress bludgeons summer resident? That's what you're here to talk about, isn't it? Where do we start?"

"'Waitress Bludgeons Summer Resident'?" Le Bel asks.

"Flora? She's in the kitchen there. She's about to serve lunch to Toad and me. Stay if you want. I don't think she'll hear us out here. I feel sorry for Flora. You know the story?"

"I've *heard* the story."

"Pemberton's Hill, yours truly with George in his new red Alfa Romeo. So I look after Flora and give her money — I mean I lend it to her." Bea lays the orange strands across her knees, smooths them, then takes a pair of shears from the canvas bag and cuts them into lengths. "Flora's husband is her problem, you'll have heard that. Dermott spends whatever I give her. The day before George died, I called her on Dermott."

Bea lifts a piece of canvas out of the bag and threads a needle. Le Bel imagines that she enjoys the role of Lady Bountiful, doling out money but controlling how her beneficiaries use it. She reaches for her glass, but it's empty. She pushes herself to her feet, spilling her canvas and strands of wool. She says, "Sure you don't want a splash? Toad, bring you a refill?" Toad lifts his glass to show it needs no attention. She totters off toward the house. Preceded by her sad little drinker's potbelly, she stumps along on her sticklike legs, reminding Le Bel of the little birds on the Wollastons' beach. She sets each foot down flat, with a hard drinker's caution, to keep her balance.

When she has disappeared into the house, Toad turns to Le Bel. "I liked George, don'tcha know, Detective," he says, "but these last years he could be a pain. Last summer we had a fire going down there on the beach, but it wouldn't burn well after the rain of the night before. He walked up to his house and came back with a pail of gasoline. When he pitched it on, the fire flared up and spread, of course, don'tcha know, and caught the tail of Margaret's coat on fire. George laughed. Margaret was scared. We all were scared. This last business, hiring that boy, I think that gave George a kick because he knew she'd worry."

Le Bel says dryly, "Let's hear it against Margaret."

The big man blinks. "Against *Margaret?*" He looks out over the flat water for a moment. "George's aunt, Constance Hardy, is a teetotaler for the most part, but she'll have a bloody Mary once in a while. One time George asked her if she'd join him for bloody Marys. She answered that she'd have a Virgin Mary and that he really should try it, without the liquor. He replied in his joyful, offhand way, 'I can't live without it.' Margaret looked utterly heartbroken. I guess nobody's a saint, don'tcha know. That's so, isn't it, Bea?"

Walking carefully, guarding her glass from spilling until it is safely on the table, Bea has come back. "Margaret?" she says as she reaches back for the armrests of her chair. "Are you asking if she's capable of killing George? What do you say, Toad?"

"People wondered why she didn't just leave him," he says. "Money of course, don'tcha know."

In the kitchen overlooking Bea's terrace, Flora replaces the orange juice pitcher in the refrigerator but leaves the vodka bottle on the counter for Bea. Behind Flora, at the kitchen table, Bea's maid sits watching TV. Two serving trays and an electric pot of fish stew are ready on the counter. In about an hour, Flora will serve lunch to Bea and Toad. For the present she leans on the low windowsill and watches the little group on the terrace.

Flora's head aches. She'd give anything for Dermott to have been more civil to the detective. She'd give anything for herself to have been. But this morning when he appeared at her door, she was tired and scared, and her feet and back hurt. She wishes with all her heart she could go back to before George's party, and do things differently.

23

JAMES AND MARGARET

James's summer job is over, so he has time to walk along the beach to Alderwood. Early frost has shriveled the ferns along the edges of the woods. Leaves on the seaside roses have turned yellow; on the smaller, wild roses, they're deep mahogany. He expects to find the porch deserted, yet he isn't really surprised to see Margaret there, sitting in her favorite chair. He clears his throat.

"Who's that?"

"It's me, Mrs. Wollaston, James."

"Oh, James. Come on up."

She enjoys sitting outdoors in overcast weather, unlike anyone else he knows. When the wind is east and other people are likely to be inside by a fire, she may be outside on the porch, bird watching or boat watching. She is a sailor; on the table she keeps a box with her binoculars and a copy of Lloyd's so that when a yacht passes, she can look up its name and owner. She likes to know where a boat was built, how old it is, and who owns it. Some skippers wait until September to sail westward toward their homeports. She likes to know who they are. The box also contains a collection of bird books — sea birds, shore birds, and land birds.

James is wearing a T-shirt and jeans for the warm weather in town. He finds Margaret bundled in a heavy, oiled-wool sweater and corduroy pants. Offshore, fog lies on the horizon like an iridescent, rolled-up blanket. Already bits of it have torn loose, unfurling shoreward on the fresh easterly wind. The air is saturated with sea damp.

"Get yourself a robe, James, out of the library."

"I'll be all right," he says. He takes his familiar seat opposite Margaret. It seems like years since he sat in one of these comfortable wicker chairs. The present moment feels odd yet comforting. George's death settles the enmity he felt, so it seems a bit like old times.

George is gone, but there's Lyle, so much like him, and he stays for the month of September. James wonders how much truth is in the rumors about Lyle and Margaret.

"How are you?" Margaret asks him.

"I'm okay. You and Angie?"

She shrugs faintly.

He adds, "How about Angie's aunt Beth?"

Margaret smiles. A pottery mug steams beside her on a table. She lifts it up and takes a sip. "You know, she isn't Angie's aunt Beth. She's Angie's aunt, but that's not her name. It's Bertha, and she hates it."

She smiles at James's raised eyebrows.

"*That's* some different," he says. It occurs to him there might be something odd in her mood. It's not like her to be drinking, although this is a good day for hot tea.

"Her name isn't Moncure either."

Disconcerted, he looks away. Out in the cove, Billy Fleet's red lobster boat is making its rounds with a cloud of gulls circling and squawking over the stern. The throb of the unmuffled engine, idling along, comes clearly across the water.

"This Mr. Moncure she talks about," he says. "He wasn't... I mean she wasn't?"

Margaret smiles. "Moncure wasn't *his* name either. His name was Murphy."

"She changed *it* too?"

"That's right."

"He didn't mind?"

"Oh no, he didn't mind anything she did. He adored her."

James says, "So she said to him, 'I'm going to call us Moncure,' was that it?"

Margaret follows his gaze down toward the water. Keeping an eye on Billy's boat, she says, "He was crazy about her, but he wasn't very nice to her. She wasn't nice to him either. They did terrible things to each other.

"When I was little, I adored them. They seemed like a prince and princess. We lived in the sticks... When they came to visit, they brought wonderful, worldly presents. They traveled and brought back Russian dolls and Spanish shawls and little painted dressing cases from Portugal.

They brought us candy in fancy English tin boxes. They loved children, but they didn't have any of their own.

"When I was your age...no, younger...I was in boarding school near where they lived. It was wonderful for me to have somewhere to go on weekends. They called their house 'The Eyrie.' It was quite beautiful, like a big playhouse. It was like a dream to be taken out by a beautiful aunt and handsome uncle, to eat at their sumptuous table, especially after boarding school fare. It gave them pleasure to have me stay with them.

"I now know it was a diversion for them because by that time they'd started to hate each other. I used to hear them arguing behind closed doors. After a while they began to make jabs at each other in front of me. I wondered why they stayed together. I was innocent enough to ask her once, 'Why don't you leave him?' Do you know what she answered? 'Because of my beautiful things.' She and I were sitting at the dining room table. She waved her hand around the room. 'I love this house,' she said. It *was* nice, full of marvelous stuff they'd collected in their travels. I understood how she would love it. I didn't know about divorce in those days of course, how hard it was for women. Uncle Paddy..."

Margaret is interrupted by a roar from Billy's boat. He has hauled his traps and is moving on at full throttle.

"Paddy?" James says as the noise diminishes.

"She called him Percival, but his name was Paddy. He had money, and he loved to spend it. She loved to help him spend it. She couldn't bear the thought of leaving that."

Margaret bends over, slides the binoculars into their box, and closes the hinged lid. "Surprised?" she says, looking up. "I was surprised, and I was upset. I loved them both. I was so young. After a while nothing they did surprised me. They went out of their way to hurt each other, and I just got used to it. I never liked it, but I got used to it."

"What happened to him?"

She doesn't respond right away. On the wind-ruffled surface of the cove, a flat trace follows Billy's wake around the point.

Abruptly she says, "Oh, he died" in a tone that conveys finality, or at least as much as she'll tell. She rises to her feet. "I have a telephone call to make. Ask Nettie to give you something to eat. No, tell her to make lunch for us both, two trays and bring them out here. I won't be long."

He stands up when she does, as she taught him. She hands him the robe from the back of her chair, warm from her back. It *is* cold, sitting here. He is bewildered: why is she uncomfortable with the topic of Mr. Moncure's death? Is she walking just a hair unsteadily, or is that his imagination? She carries the mug away with her.

He's relieved to be alone on the porch. When the door closes behind her, he sits again, staring at the woven cocoa mat on the floor. Why wasn't he more observant? On the night George died, neither Eliot nor Webber would have thought anything of his climbing up here with his flashlight. He might have learned something. Everyone assumed accidental death. He assumed it.

On an impulse he drops to his knees, places his cheek close to the floor, and sights along the boards. Too much time has gone by. Many people have walked on the porch since that night. Nettie's broom wasn't so thorough, nor that of her granddaughter Crystal, but the detective would have been thorough. And yet, if he looks hard enough, might there be something between the painted floorboards or lodged in the fibers of the mat?

During lunch, clear sky grows in the northwest, ushered along by a solid line of clouds extending to the horizon. Like a great arm, it pushes the overcast aside as it advances. As the weather clears, James watches a lone sailboat, reaching past the mouth of the cove. He can tell by the ruffled surface of the water and the attitude of the boat that there's a northwest wind blowing. Margaret taught him to read the wind this way. The scene overhead dramatically confirms the lesson.

James thinks back to his childhood wonder at such boats and the people, like Margaret and George, who own them. He used to marvel at how they could afford to summer in one place and live in another and have the luxury of moving seasonally by boat between them. He no longer envies such people.

He came to ask her a question; but he hasn't gotten around to it, as he was so distracted by the talk of Mrs. Moncure. He blurts it out: "Mrs. Wollaston, I thought you might know who my father is."

Startled, she replies, "Why, James! Why would I know that?"

"I..." Embarrassed, he stares after the disappearing sailboat. "I'm not sure. I wonder...do you think it might... I mean do you think it could have been...Mr. Wollaston?"

She gives him a disbelieving look. He sees that the idea strikes her as preposterous. "I can't imagine it, James. Whatever gave you such an idea?"

"I'm not sure." But he is sure. He's worked out the possibilities. For years he heard stories about the times George came back alone to French Haven for hunting. In Novembers when Alderwood was closed, he stayed with Eliot.

"Surely not," Margaret says after a thoughtful interval. As if she's read his mind, she adds, "He loved Maine out of season, and he was a great friend of your Uncle Eliot, but no, James, I can't imagine it. I realize your mother and Eliot are sister and brother, but I knew Mr. Wollaston pretty well."

"Do you suppose...something like that *might* have happened, and if so he'd have...known about it?"

"Would your mother have told him?"

James considers Tillie's nature and reaches his own conclusion: never. He shakes his head.

Margaret appears to have reached a conclusion. She leans toward him and touches his wrist. "He was a fair man, James. He'd have left you something. No. No, he thought of you as a nice local boy he'd become fond of."

James says quickly, "I didn't ask that to get anything out of you or Angie. It's just...Cindy says to let it rest. But I can't."

"Then let's say he *was* your father." Her expression reminds him of the old Margaret he'd first met on the beach, whom he'd loved as a child. "You and I can believe that if we want to," she says. "Between you and me. I can think of worse stepsons."

๑ ๑ ๑

Tillie, on her way out the door, turns abruptly at James's question. "George Wollaston? What're you talking about?"

"Was George my father?"

She regards him stolidly. It's a weekday afternoon; her morning shift is over. Wearing jeans and a blue windbreaker and carrying her pocketbook, she's on her way out to buy groceries. How old is she? She'll never say, but more than fifty.

He tries to imagine her before he was born, when she was in her thirties. Everyone says she was a looker. Eliot says so, and so does Nancy. She'd have been older than George by a few years but not lean and stringy like the woman standing before him now. Had they met at Eliot's house? Had George made a pass at her, and one thing led to another? What does he hope for in Tillie's answer?

"I don't know what good you think it's going to do you to find out," she says, tapping three fingers on her pocketbook.

His heart leaps — but then she goes on and it sinks back.

"It wasn't George Wollaston. It was someone you never knew. How *could* it be George Wollaston? He was the kind of summer person who'd never see a woman like

215

me. Hoity-toity! I never even met him. You ask who it was. It was a guy from Louisiana, came here two summers, stayed at that place they pulled down, down by the pier. He had a wife. I never told him about you." She pauses a moment, then throws him a rapid-fire challenge: "Are you satisfied now?"

Satisfied? *Relieved* is more the word. As if a weight has been lifted from his shoulders. "Is he...?"

"How would I know? I lost track. He never came back. Don't ask me his name because I won't tell. You have his eyes."

He stares at her while she lingers, planted in the doorway, still tapping the worn black leather of her bag.

"There," she says. "What're you going to do now? Go around telling everybody? Put a notice in the paper?"

"Not likely," says James.

24

JAMES AND ANGIE

Webber strides quickly along past the dispatcher's cubicle in the hallway of the station house. "Look at this," he says. James, Le Bel, and Chief Eliot have been talking over the case in the squad room. "This just came under the door," Webber says as he hands the chief an envelope.

Eliot opens it and scans the single sheet. He gives Le Bel a disbelieving look. "Is this on the level?" he says to no one in particular. "*Godfrey!*" He hands the paper to James.

The writing is Angie's. The folded page holds a single sentence: "I, Angie Wollaston, killed my father, George Wollaston." It was written and signed in a downward-sloping line.

"That lets *you* off," Webber tells James. He looks at Chief Eliot. "How's that for a case we thought we didn't have?"

Eliot says, "I don't know that I want to shout."

"Me neither. I like her," says James.

Eliot squeezes his chin between thumb and knuckle while he considers for a moment. He scrounged this summer job for James and bent a few rules to do it. Since hiring him he's bent a worse one: one of his regular officers was sick, so he gave James a midnight tour of duty. He'd been hired to direct traffic. *Now here's a trial for him. Let's see if he'll stay with it.* "I guess we should bring her in."

"I'll find her," says James.

Le Bel watches this exchange with an odd expression. "Ironical," George would have said. He looks at Chief Eliot and says, "Your business."

James's mind feels frozen. Nembutal; Angie, the last person he could imagine. A handful of pills in her father's drink; the Angie he knew...thought he knew. He believed the Philadelphia punk, Luke, killed George.

Angie has a few places she used to go to get away from home. One is the point that belongs to her cousins; another is the parking space above Surf Rocks out on the Shore Road. The wind is blowing hard from the east. James figures she'd go there.

In an easterly blow, the surf below the parking lot can be spectacular. With every wave that slams onto the rocks, geysers erupt, sending sheets of seawater into the air, raining torrents upon anyone standing to leeward. As James watches, a man in a red coat creeps down toward the water's edge. Preoccupied as he is, only a small fraction of his mind considers the chances of the next wave sweeping the man away. Almost subliminally he debates his own responsibility, as a police officer, for the man's safety. At least three signs are posted within a few hundred yards: "DANGER

KEEP BACK." All stand within sight of each other, of the man, and of the parking lot. There are life rings mounted on the railing with clear instructions, as if that would help.

James registers these things while he asks himself why and why, about Angie.

A gust shakes the car, and a strand of kelp hits the windshield with a hefty dollop of spray. On the other side of the parking lot is the crazy tourist's blue van. Kansas. No surf there.

From behind the van a small figure comes running, hunkered down against the wind. It's Angie. She grabs the door handle just in time to hold on through another fierce gust. By the time the gust lets up, James has unlocked her door, and in she jumps.

He is just as astounded at her sudden arrival in his car as he is about her unexpected — indeed, unbelievable — confession. He's glad to have something else demanding his attention, namely this foolish tourist.

What does James care for anyone who's stupid enough to climb down over exposed, slippery rocks to the edge of the sea in a gale, in the face of warning signs?

"Why?" he finally asks, once he's recovered his wits.

"Why?" Angie asks. "You of all people shouldn't need to ask me that."

With the wind tearing at his jacket, the man has trouble keeping on his feet in the gusts. James feels impotent and frustrated about Angie, and about the man risking his life. He pushes the car door open, but the wind presses it back. This prompts him to take his hat off so it won't blow off. He manages to get out, then hunkers down as Angie did just a moment before. He scurries forward, low to the ground against the gale, until he reaches a rock that's high enough that he can stand up and let himself be blown back against it. He waits for a lull between the ferocious gusts, then cups his hands and yells for all he's worth in the direction of the tourist, "AAAAAAAAAAY!" The man turns, startled. James waves like a windmill to urge him to come back.

The man leaves his precarious perch. The wind fills his wet parka like a sail. Up he comes, struggling to keep his footing as the wind pushes him at an ungainly trot up the uneven rocky slope.

Once the man has landed in the parking lot and manages to slow himself down, James shouts, "Don't you read signs?" He sails a bit himself, on his way back to the car. He pries the door open against the wind and crawls back in.

The cleanness of the air and the needle-like sting of spray have the same exhilarating effect on him as he's sure they have on the tourist. James takes a moment to catch his breath. He sees that Angie's fierce expression has softened a bit.

"I know, it's a joke, isn't it?" he demands. "You're just joking around with me because you don't joke with Le Bel."

"Don't be *stupid*," she says, defiantly condescending. Her tone strikes him as resigned and hopeless as well.

James counters, "Don't *you* be stupid. All you should tell them is what they ask you. Detectives are trained to listen for little things. They'll take something you don't

mean and turn it against you. Le Bel's going to take anything you say and turn it around. All that about how you
and your dad didn't get along...and the Al-Anon meetings,
he'll find stuff in that."

"Too late," she says.

She seems so strange to him, cut off, as if he and
the world around her don't exist. When he addresses her
directly, she answers in a way that suggests he has only
part of her attention. She's the one in trouble, yet it seems
he's the one who's trapped: he doesn't want to turn her in,
but he must. They circle the town, taking a long route to
the station house. Every once in a while James looks over
apprehensively at her. What's she thinking? She's come so
far. Has she screwed up again? He's afraid so.

ᔕ   ᔕ   ᔕ

Kitty arrived in French Haven at the age of nineteen.
She went to work at the French Haven Club until she found
a job as a kitchen maid in the household of Mrs. Osborne
Bassett. Over the years, she was promoted to downstairs
maid and finally reached the ultimate position of personal
maid to Mrs. Bassett herself. When Mrs. Bassett died, Kitty
inherited $30,000 and felt free to marry French Haven's
best accommodating butler-barman, Crawford.

Handsome at seventy, Kitty must have been gorgeous
in her day. She has gone back to work for the club, for she
has never in her life been idle. She met Crawford when
they both worked at the club, so this is a return to her

old stomping ground. Mrs. Osborne Bassett's daughter Bea happens to be among the club members who annually write large checks to cover the old club's alarming deficits.

Kitty hears a rumor around the club that Angie Wollaston killed her dad. She doesn't believe a word of it and berates anyone who mentions it: "I never heard such *trash. Nonsense!*"

Jack, at the bar, has been with the club since the days when Kitty and Crawford worked there. He remained Crawford's closest friend. Kitty goes in fairly early in the morning, before the forenoon lonely hearts demand his attention. "What do you make of this tale about Angie?"

"I don't care if she did confess," says Jack. "Something's wrong. She's had her hard times, we all know that, but I can't believe a girl like that would commit murder. You and I know her. You can't tell me she'd do a thing like that.

"On the other hand, if I were her, I don't know that I wouldn't have killed him."

৩   ৩   ৩

Richard remembers George teasing Mrs. Moncure and leading her on. Sometimes Richard would find the pair of them on the porch or in the sofa end of the Chinese room. Most often they'd be in the library, handy to George's bar. Each of them was apparently pleased with the other's company. George would mix himself a drink and pour a glass of sherry for her. Then he'd plop himself down on his favorite linen-slip-covered sofa and prop his feet on top of the scarred old camphorwood chest that serves as a coffee table. He'd interject short comments into Mrs. Moncure's monologue. "Is that so?" "Is that a fact?" She held her glass daintily in her small fingers and gazed earnestly into his eyes.

Margaret sometimes looked in, but she rarely joined them. Richard observed that she used the old lady as a buffer to occupy George or dispose of an unwelcome caller. The old lady's gentle rants inevitably sent visitors away. Women from the Indian reservation in Old Town came every summer to sell sweet-grass baskets and hearth brooms. In spite of the "SERVICE" sign pointing to the back driveway, they maneuvered their old Buick into the front circle to unload at the front door. They could be counted on to leave after five or ten minutes of Mrs. Moncure.

Mrs. Moncure often stood off to survey her vase of molting roses. Richard made a point of finding time to keep them fresh. "In my Eyrie," she said, "there were always flowers in every room. I endeavored to please Mr. Moncure of course. He did so enjoy flowers."

"Andrea is a young woman, not a child," she said to George one time.

"Is that a fact?" he replied.

"It is indeed a fact," the old lady assured him. "It is also a fact that there are times when it is unwise to deal too harshly with the young. Andrea has a mind of her own. The young must be led with understanding. The way must be pointed out to them."

"Is that so?" George crossed his ankles and gulped down his martini.

25

RICHARD SETS A TRAP

Richard considers the effects of the notes he gave to the police.

After he turned them in, Flora accosted him with surprising fury. What did he mean, telling the police he saw Dermott's truck there that night? "I'll work through the end of the season," she said, "because they expect that. Then you can find yourself *another* waitress!"

Margaret's attack was much less direct. No more than a remark in a deceptively mild, off-hand tone, she said, "I'm surprised you found it necessary to mention details about the furnishings in my bedroom." You of all people, she implied, who know us and our houses as well as we do, whom we trust. Her tone conveyed something puzzling. More than anger, her manner suggested perhaps it *was* fear, as he suspected before. Which was the detail that troubled her? Her open suitcase? He'd seen no reason not to mention it.

Early on a weekday morning, Angie appeared at Richard's house, where she'd never before set foot. He was amazed to see her there and staggered by her manner. She planted herself in the open doorway, hands on her hips, and gave him a cold stare. She blurted out, "Why did you tell the police the Porsche was cold?" A moment later, in a choked voice, she fired off, "I always thought you were my friend. I trusted you. Whose side are you on?" She waited implacably for an answer.

Why, indeed. Like her mother's suitcase, the information was only a detail in the pages he'd scribbled. Evidently the police distorted it to suit their purposes. It was pointless to tell Flora he never mentioned Dermott, pointless to answer Margaret at all. As for Angie, he was too taken aback to speak. Childishly, he was disappointed that she didn't seem to notice his house, didn't say, 'Wow, is this *your* place?' In the bright morning light flooding into his kitchen, he saw she'd been crying.

"Cold" was her word — or more likely that of the police lieutenant. He found his tongue at last and told Angie, keeping his eyes on her tortured face, "I didn't say your car's hard to start when it's been sitting after a drive." She relaxed at that. Richard hates confrontation, since his mother and father fought throughout his childhood.

Again he sees the night after George died: the approach of dawn in his own house; the saucepan of milk burned away and the stench of it; his fatigue and his hand cramped from writing. After he wrote those notes he felt relief, not misgivings. He had no idea what they would stir up. If he hadn't written them, he'd have forgotten the Porsche, the truck in the woods, Margaret's suitcase.

His old friend Crawford would never have made notes like that, would never, where his clients were concerned, have given information to the police. But then Crawford never had a client die on him. *He* wasn't in the house when it happened; he's dead.

෨ ෨ ෨

Richard pushes aside a badminton net, a ragged plastic tarpaulin, a sagging wicker chair, a box of croquet mallets, and a nest of empty boxes. Each object he lifts is light in weight, as expected. What he's looking for should be in plain sight, for he's seen it plenty of times on his way through these back rooms...but he can't say just where.

There it is, carefully tucked out of sight at the bottom of the heap. It wasn't out of sight before, but half buried in all the rest of the accumulated jetsam. He dislodges it and carries it into the light of the kitchen. What a gas! The mermaid is awful, really. An eerily chemical flesh-pink with black nylon lashes and a cherry-colored mouth, she's crackled with age, with golden nylon hair falling down her inflated rubber torso.

"What's that you got there, Richard?" It's Nettie calling after him. Just arriving for work, she is hobbling in from the back, carrying her shapeless old sack of a handbag. She's wearing her cardigan, nearly the same as Flora's, only several sizes larger, over her white uniform.

He acknowledges her presence but ploughs on. Through the cool, dark pantry he goes, through the dining room and into the bright morning room. Margaret and Mrs. Moncure are having breakfast at the small table by the bay window.

"What on earth?" Margaret says.

Mrs. Moncure is stunned. She shows none of the crackpot dignity, the daft starchiness that has so amused Richard. He pities her with all his heart. He likes her, even admires her. Parts of his father's favorite poem come to him, the poet's tribute to a mouse after he dug up her nest with his plough:

> *Wee sleekit cowrin' tim'rous beastie,*
> *O, what a panic's in thy breastie!*
> *Thy wee bit housie too in ruin!*
> *Its silly walls the winds are strewin'!*
> *An' nothing now to build a new one.*
> *Cozy here beneath the blast*
> *Thou thought to dwell,*
> *Till crash! the cruel coulter past*
> *Out through thy cell.*

Mrs. Moncure fixes her sad, serious green eyes brightly on him, attentive as that mouse must have been, two hundred years ago.

The mermaid is only partly inflated. She flops over Richard's forearm.

"What *are* you up to, Richard?" Margaret asks. "Put that old thing back where you found it. Put it in the trash." She raises her voice. "Nettie..."

Nettie, still wearing her cardigan, stands at the pantry door with her jaw hanging open.

"Nettie, bring us a fresh pot of coffee... Aunt Beth, are you all right?"

With an air of deliberate, acute awareness, Mrs. Moncure says, "I am very well."

Richard surveys the old lady's face as he stands holding the mermaid.

"For heaven's sake!" Margaret says.

As Richard turns to go, he hears the scrape of Mrs. Moncure's chair and the rustle of her dress as she rises to follow him.

ဪ ဪ ဪ

What is it you are supposed to do if you think you've been drugged? Keep moving. Keep on your feet, don't sit down, don't lie down. Walk.

"What is it, Richard?" Nettie asks, alarmed. "What's the matter?"

Nettie poured his coffee; it was Mrs. Moncure who handed him the cup. He slumps to the floor.

Richard hears Eliot: "You're lucky you aren't full of booze the way George was."

He's in a hospital bed, can barely move. His recall is hazy...it gradually comes back...

But Mousie, thou are not alone...
In proving foresight may be vain...
The best-laid schemes o' mice an' men
Go oft' awry...
An' leave us nought but grief an' pain
For promis'd joy!

Poor Mrs. Moncure.
Poor Mrs. Moncure indeed!

"You should've seen Detective Le Bel when he heard about this! He stopped by to congratulate you for solving the case, but you were still out of it. He said to give him a call if you ever want to change careers... Anyway, we'll soon have her locked up."

"Ah..." says Richard, unaccountably distressed.

"Don't waste your sympathy," Eliot says with a beaming smile.

26

MRS. MONCURE'S NEW EYRIE

Mrs. Moncure's old knees complain at the effort of climbing onto her cot, but she finds the result worthwhile. From the barred window, she can easily see the whole parking lot. People wearing coats are coming and going, their cheeks reddened by the cold. All in all, she reflects, she is quite comfortable. She'd prefer, of course, to stay on at Alderwood with Mellicent and Andrea and accompany them when they move back to New York. Yet she does very well. She hardly minds the confined space. She's grown used to confined spaces, even to prefer them.

She lived quite comfortably in the hotel where she knew Witherspoon. He knew where to sell her rings. He gave her the hotel's smallest room. As it turned out, she grew used to the sounds of the air conditioning machinery. Such is the effect of habituation. Witherspoon remembered what she'd told him about Tatiana and Bradford. When she fell ill, he found their number in her address book.

She's always aimed at a feeling of security, and who's to say prison is not secure? French Haven's little jail consists of only two cells, one of which is empty. Andrea was in the other cell when Mrs. Moncure arrived. It's such a pity she didn't stay. Mrs. Moncure's cell has an air of coziness — homeliness, even, with the sounds of the policemen's voices and the reverberation of their footsteps. Sometimes she sees the nice men who work at the fire department next door.

An old Buick enters the parking lot and comes to rest behind the Shop 'n' Save. At the wheel an elderly woman sits frowning. Mrs. Moncure would like to talk to her. It's clear that the woman is sad. Mrs. Moncure would say, "Nothing that life brings is intolerable. Be a philosopher! I know what sorrow is!"

"By God, Bertha," Mrs. Moncure's brother-in-law said, "call me 'Bud,' not 'Bradford'! And your sister is Thelma, not 'Tatiana'! Thelma's an old woman, and I'm an old man. We can't cater to you. Thelma's too old to put a rosebud on your breakfast tray every day. Who do you think you are?" Other passengers stared while waiting to board the bus. Bradford rattled off his parting words. "Thelma and I aren't the Ritz or wherever it was you lived with Paddy! What happened to Paddy's money? Tell me that! You never could tell what's real from what isn't! Thelma told me about you when you were a little girl!"

When Mrs. Moncure was little, her older sisters petted her, brushed her hair, buttoned her shoes, gave her their dolls, sneaked brown sugar bread for her. They loved her so, their dear baby sister. But they grew into women who allowed their husbands to escort her onto buses and trains.

Stephanie, a faded-looking woman who shared Mrs. Moncure's seat, comforted her after the bus got underway. The sight of a lady Mrs. Moncure's age being hustled onto a bus at ten o'clock at night made her want to cry, she said. She offered Mrs. Moncure half a pickle and mayonnaise sandwich out of a paper bag. Then Stephanie's Rollo, putting on the same kind of public scene, shouted, "Rollo my ass!"

So vulgar. So unnecessary.

"Just tell me where you get these crazy ideas you come up with!" Rollo shouted. "I'm Ralph! *Ralph*, Bertha! Sal can take it, she's used to you. But I'm not, and it's my house too. She's not well, and I won't have you impose on her!"

The train out of Lexington was crowded, with people standing in the aisle. A young blonde woman nudged her husband, who rose to offer Mrs. Moncure his seat. Mrs. Moncure found herself jammed in with their young family of five, traveling to Detroit. Again half a sandwich; such was the gesture these simple people offered an old lady unceremoniously put on a train by a rude, shouting old man. Jelly sandwiches. How sympathetic the young wife was! Sadly the husband was less so. One small child was in the mother's arms, and two more were asleep in the seats opposite.

Now in the parking lot, the older woman, wearing a shabby red mackintosh, leaves the Buick. Mrs. Moncure watches her turn the corner and disappear, on her way to the Shop 'n' Save no doubt. Mrs. Moncure would like to pass on to such a woman some of the kindness she has known in her own life, from the woman who offered the pickle sandwich to the woman with the young family. From Witherspoon and his daughter to Mellicent.

Mellicent made her welcome and offered her a choice of rooms. She sent that nice Nellie up to her Little Eyrie with her meals on trays.

Across the parking lot comes a girl holding the hand of a little boy with mittens pinned to his coat sleeves. Mrs. Moncure was never blessed with children of her own. It was such a great disappointment. Percival wanted them too.

Two boys toss the hat of a third boy who's trying not to cry. The world indeed is filled with sadness. Mrs. Moncure's old muscles ache from standing so long on the cot. She climbs down from the window and perches on the bedspread.

She's always been able to make herself comfortable in the smaller and smaller places she's been reduced to inhabiting after she lost Percival. Her gift all her life has been an ability to make do. It was a real shock to see the money flying away so fast and then to realize that there wouldn't be enough. She resigned herself to single rooms, quite small rooms at the last, in quite indifferent hotels. Then oh! Things got so very much worse. The money really ran out. She turned first to Tatiana, then Stephanie, then Penelope. Always at the end was the same sad, unnecessary scene. Mrs. Moncure does not believe in raised voices.

Mellicent now, such a sweet child, Penelope's only girl, grown into such a lovely young woman. Such a nice house, such a dear, dear husband; Mrs. Moncure liked Geordie. He used to tease her, but her philosophy is that a little friendly volleying between equals is a healthy thing. He reminded her of Percival.

Mrs. Moncure recognized a kindred spirit in Mellicent years ago. As a little girl, Mellicent had loved things, loved houses. Mrs. Moncure saw right away that she cherished Alderwood in the same way that she loved her Eyrie. Yet, unlike herself, poor Mellicent grew so unhappy that she neglected Alderwood.

She made all those trips with Geordie's brother, and no one was the wiser. Then Mellicent decided to leave Geordie.

ॐ ॐ ॐ

Two beautiful coverlets from Alderwood hide the nasty concrete walls. A woolly rug from Andrea's room hides much of the concrete floor. An ornament or two would be nice: a sweet-grass basket, perhaps, to keep her greeting cards in and a silk puff for her cot. Mellicent would not mind parting with one of the gold pair in the yellow bedroom.

One has to think, ridiculously, in terms of soft objects, nothing that could be used to inflict harm on one's self. Such a silly rule. No perfume, because of the glass; sachets then, scented soaps... Potpourri would be nice. She could also do with some embroidered linen hand towels, a silk-lined stocking case, and one of the small slipper chairs from the upstairs hall. The mahogany folding steps from the library would allow her to see out the window without having to climb up on the cot. They would double as a table as well! Mrs. Moncure leans back against Mellicent's filet lace pillow and thinks of other things she'd like. Mellicent would bring her almost anything, given the circumstances.

But then Mrs. Moncure is not certain that Mellicent, too, won't fail her in the end. She knows it would not be in as dramatic a manner as the others did. Rather it would be willy-nilly because she herself would be foundering and would not have the strength to keep in touch with her aunt.

Footsteps come down the corridor, and there's a jangle of keys. One of those nice policemen says, "Someone to see you, missus," and unlocks her door. She follows him upstairs to the room where they let her receive visitors.

Today her visitors are Robin and Andrea. They are holding hands. Geordie would never have approved of that. How doubly fortunate, then, that Geordie is gone!

"I've always had a knack for making myself comfortable wherever I've found myself, Robin," Mrs. Moncure says. "That nice Captain Sunderland has promised to write to me."

That'll be the day, Richard says to himself.

As for Robin's part in her being where she is, "forgive and forget" is Mrs. Moncure's motto.

27

THE TEA PARTY

Richard sets an old-fashioned tea table by the library fire. The room seems filled with sunshine. In fact it's the glow from the yellow-gold leaves of two vast Norway maples and an elm whose canopy hangs like an awning over this end of the house. It is four o'clock of an overcast October day, already drawing on toward dusk.

Angie lounges at Richard's elbow, watching him set up the table. "You know, Dad would have loved this," she says. "He loved Mom to use this table and that chair. He said it reminded him of Grandma, who loved October and stayed until Thanksgiving. She sat in that chair when she poured tea. Dad hoped someday I'd sit in it...or Tony's wife...but not Nickie. Poor Nickie! He'd have to have had a wife who'd gone to one of the great boarding schools, like Madeira or Saint Tim's." Mimicking George, with an exaggeratedly severe tone and frown on her face, she adds, "One of us."

She is wearing another Indian print, not too different from the dress she wore the night her father died. She has a pullover sweater over it and wool leggings. She sighs. "Poor Dad. I miss him. I mean I miss him the way he used to be."

She's grown up, Richard thinks as he looks at her calm face. The lines about her mouth are gone. Her face is fuller and her demeanor less agitated. "If your dad were here, there'd be rum on the tray," he says. George liked to drink rum in the fall.

"I'd accept the rum if we could have him back the way he used to be," she says. The doorbell rings. "That's Aunt Constance. I'll go."

It's Lucasta. Richard sees her in the hall mirror, haughtily drawn up, swaying slightly, bundled in a scarf, a heavy sweater, and gloves. He finishes setting up, then heads off for the kitchen. A glance out the front door as he passes shows the bundled shapes of Toad and Les Girls too as they arrive. They've been to another party, evidently. In the still air, blue smoke from the chimneys has sunk to hover around their ankles.

"We're only going to have *one* drink, Angie dear," says Lucasta. "We were just passing by and we thought we'd stop in and see how you are. Then we're taking you and your mother out. Now don't say 'no.' You can't stay in and mope forever, you know."

"Nobody's moping, Mrs. Forbush," Angie assures her. Waving a hand toward the library, she adds, "We're about to have a party. I mean Aunt Constance is coming."

Lucasta takes a firm hold of the door. Perhaps it's to steady herself, but the effect is to thoughtlessly block the others from entering. "Angie dear, you and your mother must *not* isolate yourselves," she says. "We're your friends. We're here to help. Oh, I see you have Richard. Is it a party? Did you say Miss Hardy? How nice. Well. Old friends can just come in for *one* wee drink, can't they, Angie dear?"

Lucasta pushes past Angie, bringing the chill of autumn air and the scents of wood smoke and metabolized gin. "Oh, here *is* Miss Hardy," she says, turning back to the old lady arriving on the arm of her chauffeur. She offers her hand. "So nice to see you, Miss Hardy. Lucasta Forbush — Lucasta Weems," she amends, using her maiden name, assuming she has to jog the old lady's memory.

"Weems," Miss Hardy echoes. Toad gives her his arm as she comes inside.

"Aunt Constance," Pris says, and kisses Miss Hardy on the cheek. "Margaret dear." Margaret has appeared from another room.

"Angie dear," Lucasta says, "tell your mother *she* may be having *tea* with Miss Hardy, but Richard will mix some-thing *else* for the rest of us." Lucasta is now in the hall, headed toward the library. So are Pris and Bea. Miss Hardy and Toad follow. The little group progresses together in a clot.

Toad hands Miss Hardy to a chair, then kisses Margaret and Angie. "Then the rumor's true, Angie," he says. "You're buying Andrews' Garage?"

"I'm going back to school, Mr. Cordwainer. Taking this term off, but going back."

"Not buying Andrews' Garage?" Toad looks disap-pointed. "So much gossip, don'tcha know."

"Richard, chop chop." Lucasta mimes raising a glass to her lips. She gives the tail of his jacket a tweak as he passes. "Mrs. Bassett will need a drink too."

Richard likes Lucasta, a truly remarkable lady...until she's had a drink or two, when her agreeable character undergoes a sea change. He imagines that if she could have weaned herself from alcohol she might have been a famous chef, landscape designer, or director of an arboretum.

In a stage whisper Lucasta addresses Margaret: "Where *is* the old lady?" With an embarrassed look at Miss Hardy, she amends, "I mean the other one, your aunt... Seriously."

Margaret frowns and pours from the teapot into Miss Hardy's cup.

"Sing Sing?" Bea suggests.

"She's here," says Angie. "I mean here in French Haven, in jail." The doorbell rings again. "Oh Mom, it's James." She excuses herself to go to the door. She returns with Cindy and James and introduces them. "You all remember James, Chief Eliot's nephew. This is Cindy, his fiancé.

In silence the group assesses the fact that two young French Haven natives are included in their party.

Toad clears his throat. "Have dinner with us, Maggie? After tea. A table for all of us at that new place, don'tcha know."

"Richard." Margaret lowers her voice to an undertone. "Do you think Flora might be free? Can we get some lobsters?" She turns to Miss Hardy, "Aunt Constance, you'll stay, won't you? Richard will call Agnes."

"Yes, Mrs. Wollaston," Richard says and leaves to make the arrangements.

🔊 🔊 🔊

Richard and Flora have spread the table with news-papers in lieu of a cloth, and the party has moved to the dining room. The papers are littered with lobster shells and smeared with butter as well as roe and liver, also known as *coral* and *tomalley*.

Miss Hardy beams down the length of the table. "A regular picnic," she says joyfully.

Lucasta twists off an end of bread and mashes it into the juices on her plate. "I have to pity Enid," she says.

"Pity Lucretia Borgia," Bea says thickly.

Miss Hardy takes her eyes off Bea's bosom, which is sinking steadily toward her plate. "Why do you say you *pity* Enid?" she asks Lucasta.

"You don't mean to say you haven't heard? I'd have thought the family would have been the first to know. Shall I tell?"

"Yes, do tell," Bea mutters lethargically.

"Lyle has kicked Enid out, Miss Hardy. He's going to stay on here while she packs up at home."

"Lyle?" Miss Hardy echoes. "Enid?"

"Very sad," says Lucasta. "Said he never wants to see her again. Says she's behaved badly."

"Enid?" Miss Hardy says. "She does behave badly."

Flora arrives with fresh newspapers. Soon she is back again, carrying a tray of fingerbowls.

Toad looks across the table at Margaret. "George had some awfully good cigars, don'tcha know. You wouldn't mind if after dinner James here — it is James, isn't it? If James and I help ourselves?"

Lucasta returns to her story. "You know, Enid's been vandalizing Outer Mongolia. She was so upset, she took all the light bulbs out of the sockets. Carried all the sheets and pillowcases down to the beach and threw them over the bank."

Toad looks at James. "And you're giving up police work?"

"No sir, I'm going to the academy in Waterville. Cindy's coming too."

Toad turns his prominent eyes on Cindy. "You're going to be a policewoman?"

"Yes, sir, and... James, you'd better tell them, since Angie already has."

"We're getting married," says James.

"Well, well," Lucasta observes; then after a pause, "I invited that good-looking detective to lunch. I told him he could interview us all at the same time, but he declined."

For some moments Miss Hardy has been feeling in the crevice between the cushions of her chair. Now she brings up a gleaming object between her fore and middle fingers. "Did someone lose an earring?"

"That's mine," says Bea. "I wondered where it went."

Richard feels relieved to have *that* question put to rest.

28

RICHARD AND FLORA

"If you take back all the summer places down here," Flora says, "and if you give 'em back to the people who ought to have 'em by rights, Dermott's family would own all this: Wollastons' and Bea Bassett's and Lucasta's and all them places, all the woods from here out to the bluffs and all that point and out to Pemberton's Hill and all past that, all the way to Mountpeace. That's right, every bit of it. Now my point is, someone who owned all this in the olden days has a right to the use of it. I say a man like Dermott can walk on the beaches if he wants to and pick the blueberries and cranberries and blackberries. If he wants to, he can dig clams and jack deer. People nowadays have no right to interfere. Hardestys had the land first. They settled it and took care of it. If it wasn't for people like Dermott's family, this would be woods down here, and you know what? There wouldn't be any French Haven today. Did you ever taste any of the mincemeat I make from the deer Dermott jacks right out there behind Wollastons' garage?"

Richard suppresses an urge to lift an imaginary violin to his shoulder and accompany Flora's monologue. "La la la," he'd sing. But he knows Flora too well; he holds his tongue. They've patched up their feud. She likes to work, she says, and she's used to Richard... She can't sit at home all day with Dermott, can she? As for the idea of blinding deer with flashlights, to Richard it seems unsporting. But he says nothing.

Breaking an old rule, he shares a bottle of wine with Flora after the impromptu lobster dinner. It's only half a bottle, but Flora's share is enough to set her off. Her face is flushed and her eyes shine. Richard has never seen her so animated. Dermott might give the land back to the Indians: did she say that or didn't she? Maybe it's only the wine and the heat in the kitchen.

Richard rises from the table and crosses to the open window to let the stream of night air refresh him. He has set a large container of the party's leftovers on the sill to cool. Lobster juice, shells, butter strong with lemon, bits of coral and tomalley — he carries it back to the table, tops it up, and caps it.

Flora watches absently. "The first Hardesty was born not far from where you and I are sitting. You know, I was married before. My first husband was Dermott's brother."

The kitchen, redolent of parsley and lemon and spilled wine, feels warm and pleasant. The touch of cold air has cleared Richard's head. He puts the container of leftovers near the door, ready to carry out to the Subaru, then resumes his seat. The evening seems memorable. He's never, in all his years with Flora, seen her idle. Now she sits, relaxed as a rag doll, talking her head off. So much has come full circle, he thinks; so much has changed.

"Read your history," she goes on implacably. "When the British was blockadin' Boston, Hardestys here on these islands had full cellars. They did, you can look it up. Hardestys sent help up there to Boston, saved them people's lives."

Flora's face can never be called pretty, but flushed and animated in the kitchen's bright light, Richard sees traces of the charming girl in the school photograph.

"You're in fine fettle, Flora," he teases her. "Has someone died?"

She turns abruptly toward him, with a violent look. "Someone *has* died," she says, her voice startling him with its passion. "And it's a blessing! I told you I was married before. My first husband died last night. You never knew about Tim, did you? Or no, snoopy as you are, maybe you do. What you don't know — what nobody knows — is I used to pray for him to die. All these years you thought my mind was on trimmin' asparagus, washin' lettuce, puttin' away dishes, handin' them platters around, and moppin' up. No, I was prayin'. I prayed he'd go to sleep, and the next mornin' they'd call me and say, 'Flora, Tim never woke up.' Well, yesterday he didn't wake up. And I say thank God it's over. All I wish is George was here to know it. He would've been as glad as I am. He did everything a human man could do for Tim. He never did mean to cripple him. What happened was the kind of accident could happen to anyone."

She twists in her chair to see the clock. Richard, following her glance, foresees the sequel. When Dermott arrives, no force on earth can prevent her from leaving. Unless... She seems a changed woman. He pours the last of the wine into her glass.

"Flora, when you and I finish up here, I'll take you down the street and buy us both a *real* drink."

She gives him a judgmental look. "What will Angie say?"

"What's Angie got to do with it?"

"You know as well as I do. George isn't here to say he won't have you for a son-in-law." Abruptly Flora sets her glass down. "What do you think happened to Mr. Moncure? I've been thinkin' about that. I say he died of a fall down some steps. And if they did an autopsy on him, they'd have found Nembutal, I'll bet you, just like George."

They hear the truck. "There's Dermott," she says. She drains her glass and gets to her feet. "You take *Angie* out, not me. I'm mad at him for mixin' her up in his business."

"Come on, be fair," Richard says, surprised to find himself standing up for Dermott. "Do you really think if Angie wanted to go clamming with him he could have stopped her?"

That settles her down a bit. "Well, I guess not. Good night, Richard."

He has an idea why Angie would go clamming with Dermott. He has seen her hanging out in Casey's Convenience Store. It is clear that she feels close to the workmen who go there for coffee. He understands how they'd think of her: as a rich kid who has a few problems, daughter of a man who had a few problems. They kid her; she likes to be kidded. She feels welcome with them in a way she never did with her father. She probably jumped at the chance to join Dermott. It would certainly take her mind off her current troubles. He probably welcomed her, if only to add to his catch.

Richard hears Dermott's truck roar to life and bomb off, louder and faster than usual.

Flora comes back in and eyes him anxiously. "I've left Dermott."

"*Good news!*" he exclaims.

"I told him, and he left me standing in the driveway. My sister will put me up, but I need a way to get there."

"Sure, I'll give you a lift."

ဪ ဪ ဪ

On their way out of Alderwood's driveway, Richard and Flora glimpse a familiar figure lit up by the Subaru's headlights. It's Angie, walking toward them. Richard slows to a stop.

She holds a hand up against the glare of the headlights. She walks around to the passenger door and peers in.

"Flora? That you? Dermott forget to pick you up?"

"Weren't you ridin' with James and Cindy?" says Flora.

"I wanted to walk. I asked them to drop me off."

"Well, I want to talk to you," says Richard. "Hop in."

She opens the back door and climbs in. "Get that," she says ironically. "He says he wants to talk to me."

Flora twists around to face her. "I left Dermott."

After a momentary silence, Angie exclaims, "For God's sake, Richard, let's take her someplace and celebrate."

"You celebrate for me," Flora says. "I need to get off my feet."

They stop by her sister's neat little house on Everard Street. Flora takes her bag and gets out. Angie gets out and climbs in next to Richard.

Flora calls up to one of the upstairs windows, "It's me, Flora."

Angie tells Richard, "I find this fascinating. You want to talk to me? Here I am."

"Not here," he says.

A light has come on in the upstairs room, and a head appears out the window. "Well, *my land!*" The head ducks back inside. Nearly right away, lights come on downstairs and then on the porch.

Walking toward the porch steps, Flora turns and calls back, "You two go on."

A woman in a bathrobe opens the door. "What's all this?" She steps back to make room for Flora, who waves at the car and enters the house. The door closes, and the porch light goes out.

"So?" says Angie. "Where to?"

"How about the Shore Road?" says Richard.

"You mean *park*? You want to neck with me? Oo-ooo, Richaahd!"

He feels exhilarated, but very awkward. So many changes, so much that's new. He makes a U-turn and drives back the way they came, through the sleeping town. Most of the shops and restaurants have closed for the season. Only a few motels show lighted "VACANCY" signs, hoping for trade from those who come for the fall colors. Out they go through the town's dark, outlying streets, past the darkened cottage driveways. The view opens out as they enter the Shore Road. No moon, no stars. In the darkness, Richard feels rather than sees the sea. He enters a turn-off labeled "SCENIC LOOKOUT." The headlights show another car beside the granite boulders lining the parking area. Richard feels both elated and ridiculous. A man nearing thirty, he has utterly missed the popular culture of his generation. Now here he is, about to park like any kid in a dark lovers' lane with a girl eleven years younger than he is. He's about to enter the rites of teenage courtship.

"This is *some romantic*, Richaahd," Angie says in her heaviest Down East accent. She seizes his hand. "You're not afraid you'll lose control? If you're going to say what I think you are, I'll help you out. Remember I said once if you weren't so old, I'd marry you? Well, I'm ready to make the sacrifice."

"That makes it easy," he says, "but what about auto mechanics school? You weren't serious about that?"

She gives his hand a squeeze. "What do *you* think? That was to get Dad's goat."

"Well it worked... What about at the party just now when you told everyone you'll be going back to school?"

"Oh, I was just playing with them, telling 'em what they wanted to hear."

Silence descends. The ghosts of George and Richard's father have come between them. The Reverend Andrew Grassie used to harp on what he called "holy chastity" with poignant, guilt-laden admonition. The memory won't let him be; he has never really been able to get past it.

Angie soulfully sings, "Shame, shame, shame..."

"What?" says Richard, returning from his reverie.

She continues, "Shame of fools..." It helps to break the ice.

Angie says abruptly, "I see I'm going to have to help you out. I just made you a serious proposal. I bet you've got a sock-full stacked away, and I'm about to have some money of my own. How about we set up a catering shop? Get you out of your monkey suit, get me into the kitchen. We do the brain work. We hire people like Flora and some of the college kids who want summer jobs. We hire your competition. How about it?"

29

RICHARD AT ELIOT'S

Richard reflects on the evening when Eliot invited him home for supper. It was soon after Mrs. Moncure found herself in a new home. It appeared that Richard had solved the case, and Eliot asked him to sum it up for him.

Richard parked in a spot opposite the police chief's house on South Street. He reflected on how Eliot is such a different type from himself. He's the perfect insider, a man whose family has been established in French Haven for at least as long as Maine's written history stretches back. Eliot was a popular athlete in school, a football player and a local hero, according to Josephine. She and her schoolteacher father had arrived here when she was small, so she came to feel she was a part of the community.

Richard, however, is an outsider. He comes from away, as the saying goes. Ministers' families are like military families, it seems to him: always moving on. If Andrew had lived longer, would he have brought Clara and Richard to a town like this in Canada? Richard imagined himself having grown up in a Canadian counterpart of French Haven, with the same sense of belonging as Eliot Perham or at least Josephine. Nevertheless Richard, a lonely boy uprooted from a shaky background, has grown into a reserved man who has slowly established himself in French Haven.

He felt proud, getting out of his car in front of Eliot's house. He was a guest to be welcomed at the door, fed a meal at the family table, and allowed to learn to know this local couple in their own house. He was also apprehensive: what gaps, if any, would the chief notice in his story?

Nancy greeted him at the door. "I don't know how *my* cooking's going to taste to *you*. Eliot eats it, so does James, so did our kids. Well, I recognize you from around town. I'm glad to meet you. He's in there watching the news."

Richard liked the homey, closely packed living room with its plain maple side tables, big TV, and Eliot's brown vinyl lounger. Not a book in sight.

Pot roast and vegetables, coleslaw, pie, and coffee: the plain, well-cooked, and simply served meal was a treat to Richard. Not since his childhood had anyone cooked for him — not even Crawford, not even Josephine...except breakfast after George died. Eating a family meal with Eliot and Nancy made him realize what a loner he was, and how lonely.

When the meal was over and the table cleared, Nancy excused herself. She was going to go over to her mother's house. She'd just slip out while they were talking and not interrupt. If Richard happened to still be there when she came home, fine. If not, it was nice having him. She trusted he'd cook for her and Eliot someday at his place. He and Eliot moved back into the living room, and they heard her cleaning up behind the closed kitchen door.

There was no fire in the wood stove on its red-brick hearth, but the furnace was turned up high. "She likes heat," Eliot said after pushing himself to his feet to lower the thermostat.

"Flora was scared that maybe Dermott killed George," he said as he settled back down. "For running down his brother and all. But Dermott was clamming at the time. And Angie saw him at it and joined in! Old Dermott sure took some risk on a night with the moon like that."

"He did," said Richard. "Anyone in a boat would've noticed. Anyone out walking around the other cottages would have. And think of it: Flora on her feet all day, then sitting for two hours in that old truck."

From the kitchen came the sounds of the dishwasher starting and the back door opening and closing.

Richard had rehearsed what he intended to say and what he'd leave out. "I decided it wasn't Flora. She was *tired*...and she's scared of the dark. I figure she'd never leave that truck for anything till Dermott came back. I didn't believe Angie when she said she did it. I didn't believe Margaret either. That whole business was ridiculous — comical really, if it weren't so sad."

"Yes," said Eliot. "When we got Margaret's confession so soon after Angie's, it was pretty clear what that was about. No mother wants to see her daughter locked up for murder. You didn't want it to be them, and neither did I.

Margaret's a nice woman, in her way. I give her high marks for having put up with George."

"Now, about that night," Richard continued, "when I went out on the porch, when I found George's body. I'd been indoors all night. Coming out on the porch, I smelled flowers. You know how it can be with that kind of wind in the summer, all the land smells you get even if you're out on the water. I thought of gardens and woods, but later on something else dawned on me. Mrs. Moncure wears different perfumes. She had a dozen or so little bottles up there on her dressing table. That got me thinking about *her*."

"Yeah." Eliot twisted his face into a grimace. "She's been after me to let her have some of that stuff at the station house."

"Poor Mrs. Moncure," Richard said. "She's run out of relatives. Margaret and George were her last stop. When she got there, she figured she was all set. I guess Margaret had the space and, in her predicament with George, having a guest would be a welcome distraction. Then Margaret said she was going to leave him." At least, Richard figured, Mrs. Moncure certainly overheard Margaret saying, "I'm leaving you, George" after his blowup with Angie. She must have told Mrs. Moncure later as well.

"When I went to New York, I found an old lady Mrs. Moncure had mentioned to me — said her father had been good to her once. Witherspoon, Mrs. Moncure said his name was. Of course it turned out to be something else: Weinstock. After Mr. Moncure died, Mrs. Moncure lived in hotels. Then money got tight. By the time she met Mr. Weinstock, she was holed up in a 'little fleabag hotel,' as the old lady put it, 'way downtown.' Weinstock was the desk clerk. Finally, when Mrs. Moncure couldn't afford even that, she started on her final travels, looking for a home with her relations. Before she left she asked Weinstock if he'd hold some stuff for her till she got settled. He agreed, but then he died. His daughter got the stuff, books and papers mostly, including newspaper clippings about Mr. Moncure's death. Guess what he died of. A fall down a flight of stairs. There was no autopsy, and he was cremated.

"When Mrs. Moncure couldn't talk Margaret out of leaving George, she was desperate. Mrs. Moncure's an insomniac, takes Nembutal every night — one pill, sometimes two. So she got the idea about the pills and the mermaid. She came downstairs to check around to see where everyone was. That was when Lucasta saw her, but she was too drunk to remember. Mrs. Moncure propped the mermaid in her chair by the window so it would look like her own shadow on the window shade as usual when she's up in her room reading. She put a few pills in her pocket and came down to sit with George on the porch. She sneaked the pills into his drink and stayed till she was sure he'd drunk it. Then she probably took the glass and washed it. The next morning she must have put the glass back in the bar. I looked everywhere for that glass. I figure the detective didn't find it either."

Eliot's expression became increasingly grim. "Anyway, we've got her locked up now," he said. "And about the suitcase, a woman about to leave a man isn't going to kill him."

"Right," said Richard, watching Eliot's face. It was Eliot who said it, not Richard.

30

RICHARD AND MARGARET

Richard and Margaret are alone after a simple, early dinner with Miss Hardy by the library fire. He watches her leave her chair to sit on the club fender that surrounds the hearth. She bends down, takes the fire tongs, pulls together the smoldering embers, and builds up the fire in anticipation of Angie's return. He senses she wants something more from him.

His policy, instilled by Crawford, is never to address his clients unless they address him. But he takes the liberty of asking, "Mrs. Moncure will be all right, Mrs. Wollaston?"

She hangs up the tongs and resumes her seat in one of the leather chairs drawn up to the fender. "The law may be lenient, considering her age. At least we hope so. She was delighted that you went to see her."

"Mrs. Moncure and I are friends," he says.

The single time he called on her, Mrs. Moncure seemed unchanged. He was most impressed that without a hitch, she resumed her usual monologue as if nothing had changed between them. It was as if she weren't in jail and he had not been the means of putting her there.

Margaret gets up again to brush the hearth and return the brush to its stand. The rest of the room is tidy. Richard's work in the kitchen is nearly finished. All that remains is to wash the punch bowl and cups. He picks them up but lingers. He still senses she requires more of him.

She lifts her glass of water and studies the pattern etched in its side. "There's one thing I don't understand, Richard," she says. "That night, how did you notice the gate was open?"

"I happened to look when I was checking the living room before I went home. With the moon, everything was so bright. Of course I saw it."

Frowning, she revolves the glass in her hand as a connoisseur might do. Over its rim her eyes meet his. "Of course."

An ember crumbles in the fireplace. Richard's train of thought is spurred on by her words: "of course." Of course he checked the front of the house one last time before he left for the night: she knows him well enough. And there was the moonlight; anyone would have been stopped by it. She'd counted on that.

Of course.

What of the earphones? She's a non-tech person, he believes. She'd provided herself with them, perhaps borrowed from Angie's room, because she knew what was about to happen on the porch. She wanted to blot out a sound she hadn't the courage to face. Richard couldn't explain the shawl she had around her on that warm night. She was ready for something; she was expecting a knock on her door. For a woman of her upbringing, expecting a knock at her bedroom door by a *servant* is indicative of something extraordinary indeed!

Of course.

She knew Richard was still in the house. She'd made sure, before telling him "good night" in the kitchen, that George was marooned on the porch. George would be forced to go down those steps because she had locked him out there.

Of course.

The suitcase? A woman about to leave a man wouldn't kill him; Eliot said that. She had intended to leave George, until another option occurred to her.

ॶ   ॶ   ॶ

Mrs. Moncure, in her new Eyrie, reminisces about the events that led to poor Geordie's unfortunate downfall. She liked Mellicent's Geordie so much! Who could have foreseen the change in him, or in Mellicent? Everyone knew that Geordie drank, but no one suspected Mellicent: she's clever. Mellicent's only soft spot is her children. Andrea's confession came close to ruining everything.

It started as a joke, when Mrs. Moncure told Mellicent, "You look murderous this morning, my dear."

"I *feel* murderous, Aunt Beth," answered Mellicent, near tears. Mrs. Moncure's heart went out to her! They continued, grimly joking, for weeks on end. Then it turned serious. Little by little, they chose roles.

"No one will suspect someone my age," Mrs. Moncure said one day, and Mellicent laughed. "What about Robin?" Mrs. Moncure asked.

Mellicent said, "He may figure something out, Aunt Beth, but I can handle him."

The next day Mrs. Moncure decided that the time had come. The best part was the mermaid, and it would be so easy to carry her. Folding the sleeping capsules in a hankie would be simple, same as taking Geordie's glass away and washing it afterward.

As soon as Mrs. Moncure saw that gate open, she understood. Gate open, door locked, Geordie out there by himself, drinking. She wasn't the only one to decide that night to solve poor Mellicent's problems. Oh no. She'd lock the door again on her way back in.

If Mellicent had left Geordie, he would have gone on drinking, hardly realizing that she was gone. Mrs. Moncure and Mellicent and Andrea would make do in some temporary place. It might have taken years to settle. As for Mrs. Moncure, she hasn't so many years left. She felt suddenly *so* tired, less and less able to make do. But she knew how to proceed, no hesitation. She inherited her courage and resolution from her pioneer stock.

ॐ ॐ ॐ

Richard sets the punch bowl back down. His hands are trembling. In another moment he'd have dropped it. Margaret watches him with a wry expression.

She locked George out; then she simply allowed the inevitable to occur. What she wished for but hadn't the courage to do herself, her aunt would do in her stead. She didn't wish to make the discovery, so she foisted that off on Richard.

It wasn't collusion but merely Margaret's guess at motivation. She understood her aunt. Whether or not she knew her husband's fate wasn't germane. A spur-of-the-moment act, it was suggested by opportunity, triggered by humiliation, and urged on by the moon.

Margaret set the stage. Mrs. Moncure acted deliberately. No talk between them, no plan, only, "I'm leaving him, Aunt Beth." She understood the effect the words would have on her aunt.

There's Lyle to consider as well. The two brothers were so alike, aside from the question of sobriety. Had Lyle become the George with whom Margaret had fallen in love? Did she have trysts with Lyle? Mrs. Moncure would know... Why not simply leave George and marry Lyle?

It might have been done, but, given Enid's nature, Lyle's divorce would certainly be drawn out and dirty. One divorce would be better than two, especially of the contested and indubitably publicized variety. Considering George's condition and Mrs. Moncure's predicament, it seemed a simple and inevitable unfolding of events.

Mrs. Moncure as hit man: Richard laughs.

"What's so funny?"

He shakes his head. "Nothing, Mrs. Wollaston."

Margaret's confession was interpreted as that of a brave mother taking the blame for her child. In fact it was only a belated coming forward of the guilty, without risk; she knew she wouldn't be believed.

You've guessed, haven't you? Margaret's gaze conveys. *Now you* really *know. You, the son of a drunk, have picked up on things others wouldn't. What are you going to do about it? Nothing, because you love Angie.*

The brass shovel falls with a clank on the hearth, startling him from the surreal intensity of the moment. Flustered, he dashes to retrieve it and set it back on its hook. Richard then assumes a stance taught to him by Crawford, a posture of reserve and readiness, his hands clasped loosely behind him. He is always calmed by the restful alertness of the pose.

But he is sweating. In all his conjectures, he has never dreamed of being handed such confidence, such responsibility. What does she want of him?

He senses what it is: *You want Angie. She's yours, on my terms.*

Is it as easy as that?

The library clock strikes eight. An instant later the hall clock concurs. The brass ship's clock, in George's study, joins in. The clocks are being wound again.

"Shall I check the doors before I go, Mrs. Wollaston?"

"Please do, Richard, thank you," she says. "I think I'll sit up a while longer. Angie has her key."

Angie has her key. The same words she said that night.

"Good night, Richard. Thank you. You always do a wonderful job."

"Thank you, Mrs. Wollaston. Good night."

His face feels hot. The porch doors are unlocked; he opens one to find a cool breeze blowing. He steps out a moment to let it cool him off.

"I know who I can depend on, Richard," she says, the sound of her voice distorted by the wind in his ears. His scalp tightens at the eerie feeling that he's heard a ghost.

"Richard?"

A shadow dims the light that shines out from the hall. It's Flora.

"Come on out," he says.

She stops just outside the doorway, staring out. Perhaps she senses the same thing he does. She hugs herself, shuddering. "He'd have been a goner no matter what, wouldn't he?"

"George? I guess so, sooner or later." Richard imagines he hears George laugh.

At his side, Flora also peers around in the dark. "It's just that vine, scraping the eaves," she whispers tentatively.

Made in the USA
Middletown, DE
27 March 2015